MICHELANGELO

To Patricia

MICHELANGELO

MICHAEL MULLEN

With best wishes

Michael Mullen

POOLBEG

Published in 1994 by
Poolbeg Press Ltd,
Knocksedan House,
123 Baldoyle Industrial Estate,
Dublin 13, Ireland

A catalogue record for this book is available from the British Library.

ISBN 1 85371 414 3

Cover illustration by Moira MacNamara
Cover design by Poolbeg Group Services Ltd
Set by Poolbeg Group Services Ltd in Garamond 11/13
Printed by The Guernsey Press Company Ltd,
Vale, Guernsey, Channel Islands.

For Arthur Armstrong RHA

About the Author

Michael Mullen was born in Castlebar in County Mayo. He was educated in Waterford and at University College, Dublin. He has published many books for adults and children, including the best-selling *The Hungry Land*. He is particularly interested in writing for young people. *Michelangelo* is his tenth children's book for Poolbeg.

By the Same Author

Marcus the School Mouse

The First Christmas

The Viking Princess

The Little Drummer Boy

The Caravan

The Long March

The Flight of the Earls

The Four Masters

To Hell or Connaught

Chapter 1

Beneath them lay the city. They had been riding since morning and their horses were tired. It had been a long journey from Carrara with its great quarries of white marble.

"That is Rome," the father told his son Andrea.

The boy studied the sacred city. Great walls, thick and firm, stood about it. Towers and church domes rose above the red tiles of the houses in magnificent splendour. The streets seemed narrow and conspiratorial and fed into great and little squares.

This was the heart of sacred power. Men and women from all over the world came to this city in search of solace and privilege.

Saints had lived here as well as emperors and tyrants. Rome had a long and religious history. Rome had a long and sinister history. Andrea had not seen so vast a place before.

The River Tiber ran through Rome like a grey serpent. During the summer the water was low and sluggish. The stench was fetid and malarial. Every morning some murdered body was seen floating towards the port of Ostia or lying in a stagnant pool.

People were used to the sight of such things and continued about their business. The city rubbish was cast into the river where it putrefied.

"A Christian and a pagan city. It has had a dark and a bright history," the father said.

"And what of the Pope?" the boy asked.

"I will not utter a word against the Papacy but there is little resemblance between Saint Peter and Julius II. Peter, the fisherman, was poor but this Pope is richer than a king. He eats well and enjoys the finest wines. He handles a sword easier than he carries a cross."

While the father was talking he opened his hempen bag and gave Andrea some bread and cheese. His father drank wine from a leather bottle. He worked in the Carrara quarries. His hands were tough and scarred and his muscles firm.

"I already fear the city, father. I would prefer to be at home in Carrara working in the marble quarries with my family. I understand the quality of marble; I know the ring of the healthy block and the dull sound of the useless one. I know how to dress the stone with my iron chisels."

"Of course you understand marble, like all your ancestors. But you have been given a gift. You can see the vital image within the cold block. You will never be satisfied working on the surface of stone. That is why I brought you to this city. Below you lives Michelangelo. He too worked in the marble quarries. He is the greatest sculptor in the world. He will teach you the art of marble."

"But will he receive me into his workshop?" the boy asked.

"That is in the hands of fate or my good friend Giovanni, the mason. You have met him. He comes to the quarries once a year to purchase marble."

"Is he a friend of Michelangelo?"

"Yes. I believe he is."

The horses neighed in terror. Andrea saw a snake in the faded grass. He took his stick and killed it.

"Let us move forward. Tonight we stay with Giovanni. He lives in the masons' square and has a workshop there."

They mounted the horses. The horses were old and well-tempered. They moved down the hill towards the city. The sun was now high in the sky, beating down upon them. They moved through a vineyard where the lustrous grapes were ripening in the sun. It was empty. It was siesta time and the workers were asleep in small thatched huts with windows and doors open to catch some small cooling breeze.

Andrea and his father were tired and drugged by the heat. No words passed between them. They followed the dusty road to the city. Reaching a small plain, they urged the horses forward towards the Porta Latina. There they studied the stout walls thrown about the city. Clearly Rome was more than a sacred city protected by angels. Passing through the gate they entered the city.

They were amazed at what they saw. They had never seen a place as filthy as Rome. Rotting rubbish was heaped in public places. The stench was unbearable. The streets were narrow and the houses falling apart. A black mass of flies buzzed above the decaying refuse. Mangy dogs foraged for food.

"The churches may be beautiful but the streets are

ugly," the father told Andrea. "Florence on the other hand is a beautiful city. Lorenzo de Medici had taste and the Florentines take pride in their city. Rome cannot compare with it. Michelangelo worked in Florence. It was there he carved his great statue of David. It is one of the wonders of the world."

They continued to ride through the tangle of streets. As they passed into the heart of the city they became wary of the Romans. They possessed evil eyes. They were hostile towards strangers.

"Let us hold firmly to our possessions," the father advised. "This is a den of iniquity. Keep your eyes keen."

No sooner had he uttered the words than they heard a call.

"Thief! Thief! A thief has stolen my money!"

The cry was of little use. The thief disappeared down an alleyway.

People went about their business. They took such incidents for granted.

Andrea and his father moved through the crowd now filling the streets after the siesta. The city was disappointing. Everywhere it seemed to have fallen prey to decay and neglect.

They arrived at a small square. In the centre stood a fountain and the water fell musically into a marble basin. They removed their cotton shirts and washed the dust and sweat from their bodies. Then they studied the fountain. It had been carved from marble.

"Feel how fine it is," the boy said as he ran his fingers across the surface.

The father studied its shape and texture. "It is very old. It must have been here since ancient times. All over the city there are ancient statues. The people have little regard for them. The Pope and the cardinals purchase them when they are discovered. They lie buried beneath the city. People come upon them by chance."

"So there is an old city beneath the new?"

"Yes. Filled with treasures if all were known. Yet they say that the work of Michelangelo is equal in quality to anything carved by the ancient Greeks and Romans. That is what I heard from the stone cutters and the masons, and they have a good eye for quality."

"I would like to meet him."

"You will if I can help it and we will show him your work."

"Perhaps what I do is worthless?"

"I believe you have been given a gift to carve fine statues and so does every mason in the Carrara quarries. My friend will introduce us to Michelangelo. He understands the ways of the city and he has contacts here."

The heavy heat had passed and a light breeze blew through the streets. They came to the Tiber. The water level was low and a stench came off the river. Andrea studied the river. He was disappointed with it. It seemed of little consequence.

Finally they arrived at the masons' square. Here Giovanni lived with his family and with the other masons and carvers. The houses stood about the square. The masons worked under cotton awnings. They wore only sandals and light trousers.

The boy grew excited at the music of chisel on marble. It had a ring with which he was familiar ever since he could remember. He understood the mason's work. He recognised the white marble. It was from the quarries of Carrara and it had been hewn from the rocks by his uncles and relations.

"This is where the blocks are finished," his father said as they entered the square.

"I like this place. Here I will learn the art of the sculptor," Andrea said excitedly.

"No. Here they make steps and balustrades and gravestones. They are tradesmen. You must remember that you are a sculptor and you will learn your trade in an artist's workshop. That is why we have made the long journey."

"I would like to spend some time here," the boy said.

"If Michelangelo refuses to take you on as an apprentice, you can remain here. The experience will serve you well."

Andrea felt at home in the masons' square. Suddenly a voice called to them. It was Giovanni. He had been carving acanthus leaves on a marble column. He lay down his chisel and hammer and came to meet them.

"You are welcome to Rome," he said. "How long did you spend travelling?"

"Ten days."

"Did you meet any thieves on the road? The countryside is crawling with bands of soldiers. There is constant danger."

"The only thieves we met were hanging from trees."

"There is no end to the Italian wars and the soldiers have no regard for human lives. But come with me. You are thirsty after the journey. You must have a glass of wine and eat some bread and cheese. I am certain that you are starving. I have always been treated with hospitality at Carrara. Now it is my turn to return your kindness."

They sat at a long table with a rough surface,

scored with chisel marks and covered with fine white dust. It was shaded with canvas and they could view the square and the workers.

Giovanni called on his daughter Maria to serve them. Like her father she had dark hair and fine olive skin. She possessed an air of confidence.

"Is this your first time to visit the city?" she asked Andrea.

"Yes," he said shyly.

"Then you will find it a strange place. I shall show you about. I know its marketplaces and back streets better than most."

"Thank you," Andrea said.

She placed a bottle of wine before them and a large plate of bread and cheese.

Giovanni poured two goblets of wine.

"To your good health," he said raising the goblet.

As they drank the wine and ate the food they looked at the activity of the square. The masons were working to their own rhythm. There was a fine mist of white marble dust about them and white chippings lay about the bases of the marble blocks.

"I would like to work with them," Andrea said. He had little interest in the conversation of his father and Giovanni.

"Very well. Try your hand at some column or other."

Andrea walked to the centre of the square. An old man was carving a slender column of marble. Andrea stood beside him and observed him at work. He had a fluent, easy stroke.

"What is your name?" the old man asked, stopping to wipe the sweat from his forehead.

"Andrea."

"And where did you come from?"

"Carrara."

"Then you should understand marble."

"I like working with it."

"And do you know the music of marble?"

"Yes. I learned the tone and ring from my father and my uncle."

"Then what do you think of this block?" the old man asked, smiling.

The boy took the mallet and tapped the stone.

"It is of poor quality. There are bubbles in it and I do not like its colour."

"Good. I agree with you. Now let me see you work with it."

The boy took the mallet and the chisel. He weighed them in his hands.

"These are too heavy for me. One should work only with tools which are well balanced and of proper weight. I will fetch my own."

Excitedly he ran over to where his horse was tethered. He opened one of the sacks on his back and returned with his instruments wrapped in canvas. He set out the instruments which his uncle had forged for him. Picking the one most suitable to the work, he immediately began to continue where the old man had left off. His strokes were sure and confident.

The masons and their apprentices left down their tools. They came and stood about the boy. They were amazed at his ability. He had an eye for the grain of the stone and he could work with it. They had never seen anyone so young work so confidently with marble.

"You should become a sculptor," the old man said with admiration. "Some of us are born to work on the surface of marble. Others have the gift of giving it life."

"That is why I came to Rome. I wish to work with Michelangelo. My father said that he is the greatest sculptor in the world. Do you know him?"

"Of course I know him. Sometimes he visits us and examines the blocks that are carried to the square. He has a sharp eye for a good piece of stone and runs his fingers along it in search of flaws. He is a stone mason as well as a sculptor and sometimes spends a day working with us. He is not like the others who hold their noses in the air. Many artists in Rome hate him but he is one of us and we respect him."

Andrea worked with the old man for two hours. They talked knowledgeably of marble and the old man told him several interesting stories of old masons who were long dead. He had travelled all over Italy and had been to the great cities. They did not notice the long shadows of evening fall on the square.

"It is time to wet the marble and cover it with damp sacking. Many a good block of marble has cracked during the night because it has been left exposed," the old man said.

The sounds of mallets on chisels and chisels on marble began to diminish. Soon the square was silent. Men wrapped their tools in cloth wallets and bound them with thongs.

"Always respect the tools of your trade," the old man said as he placed his chisels in their cloth pockets. He had gaunt cheeks and wiry arms. Andrea would have loved to carve his head in marble. It possessed great character.

They went to a fountain and washed the fine marble dust from their hair and their bodies. Then they sat at the long bench and ate pasta prepared by Maria. They washed it down with cheap wine. They sat and talked about the city, particularly the attempts made by the Pope to beautify it. A Pope with artistic leanings would provide the masons with work. They had great confidence in Julius II.

"The city needs such a man. He may be as tough as leather but he has an eye for a beautiful building. Rome needs a master hand and we have one in the Pope," Giovanni said.

Since his election, the masons were in more demand. They did not have to travel from the city in search of work.

Night came and lanterns were lit in the windows of the houses set about the square. Soon only Giovanni and his family, together with Andrea and his father, remained.

Maria came and sat with them. She entered the conversation and had much to say about Rome and the work of the masons.

"This Pope has been good to us and I will not have harsh words said against him," she told them.

"With you on his side, Maria," her father said, "he should fear his enemies." Then he turned to Andrea's father. "Tomorrow we will try and meet Michelangelo. But now we must sleep. Carving marble is a tiring business and draws the energy from a man," he said.

The square was silent. Great pulsing stars spread across the sky like precious stones. Only the sound of water falling into a basin broke the silence. They heard a dog bark and the voice of a woman giving out to her husband.

They entered the house. It was warm inside. The stones still retained the heat of the sun. Andrea and his father made their way up a rickety stairs to the attic. They lay on straw and drew thick blankets over their bodies. Soon Andrea's father was asleep. But Andrea could not sleep. Tomorrow he would meet the greatest sculptor in the world. He would have to show him the piece of marble he had carved in Carrara. He wondered if Michelangelo would accept him into his workshop.

In the distance he heard a young man playing on a mandolin. He was singing a love song. He listened to the sweet music for some time. Then he fell into a deep sleep.

CHAPTER 2

At dawn the next day, Giovanni together with Andrea and his father, left the house. The sun lay on the eastern horizon and the air was cool and sweet. The peasants were arriving from the countryside with fruit and vegetables. The sound of great wheels could be heard on cobblestones.

They walked along the Tiber until they came to the bridge leading to Castel Sant' Angelo. They crossed the bridge. They noted how well the stones had been carved by masons long dead. Andrea remarked on how strong and wide the castle appeared.

"If the Pope is attacked by his enemies he can take refuge there. It would be impossible to dislodge him," Giovanni said.

"And has Pope Julius enemies?" Andrea asked.

"Not only has he enemies in Italy and France but there are enemies in his very court. He is a warrior

Pope and intends to win back the Papal States. He will lead his troops in battle if necessary."

"But I thought that the Pope should have no interest in war," Andrea remarked.

"Rome teaches you many things which you would not otherwise know," Giovanni told him.

Eventually they came to the quarter in which Michelangelo lived. Beside the gate which led to his walled yard, an old man sat on a marble form sunning himself in the morning light. He was heavy and had a shining bald head.

"You seek the great man himself?" he asked.

"Yes," Giovanni said.

"Michelangelo is in the yard if you are looking for him. You can enter by the wooden gate. He is always in the yard. Sometimes at night I hear him carving by lantern light. For so small and thin a man he has great power. He also possesses a bad temper. But he has a kind heart."

They opened the gate and entered. They saw a small muscular man with a crooked nose working on a statue. Andrea had expected somebody more impressive. Michelangelo was dressed like a stone mason. He did not observe them, but continued at his work.

Andrea had never seen a stone carver as clever at his task as Michelangelo. He worked the grain of the marble in long even strokes. When he was satisfied with his work, he left his mallet and chisel aside. He rubbed the dust from the marble and felt the surface with his fingers. He was about to begin again when he saw the three figures.

"Ah Giovanni. You are welcome. Have you found me a healthy block of marble to carve?"

"No. But I have brought something which you might like to see."

"Very well," he said. He took a vessel and drank some water. "Carving is thirsty work," he said, coming toward them. Andrea noted how intelligent and bright his eyes were. There were creases and lines etched around his eyes.

Giovanni opened his bag and took out a thin square of marble. The Madonna's face was chiselled on it. He handed it to Michelangelo. The sculptor examined it carefully.

"It is a fine piece of work, well carved, but not firm enough. It is the work of a young man. Who carved it?"

"Andrea." said Giovanni, nodding in Andrea's direction. "He works with his family in the quarries at Carrara. I believe that he has a gift but needs to be trained."

Michelangelo looked at the boy with his incisive eyes. "You have been granted a great gift. You must make good use of it," he said.

"Then I would like to become your apprentice. There is much that I have to learn," Andrea said quickly.

"You choose a difficult craft and there is no great wealth in it. If you wish to make money you should carve altars or tombs. Look at me – barely enough money to feed myself. The Pope invited me to Rome from my beloved Florence and since I came he has not given me a commission. He refuses to meet me. I should return to a civilised place. I do not like it here. It is full of plots and intrigues. Even the artists are rogues." There was anger in his voice.

"But others are well treated by the Pope and cardinals," Giovanni said.

"They are. I would not call them sculptors. They are toadies. They stand about the Pope, attend his fabled dinners, carve dull statues and are highly paid and praised for their work. But I am not a yes man. That is why I am poor and neglected."

"I care not for money. I will work for nothing. I wish to breathe life into stone," Andrea said.

"Like God breathing life into clay," the sculptor laughed.

"Yes," the boy said firmly.

"Then you can remain with me. But I warn you – I am not an easy master."

"But you are the greatest of sculptors," Andrea replied.

"You have a quick mind. If you do not like the conditions here, you will be free to leave."

The boy was overjoyed.

Michelangelo turned to Andrea's father.

"I know Carrara well. The finest of marble is quarried there. I have visited it many times. One of these days I intend to go there again."

"Then you are welcome to stay at my home. It is a modest place but we will feed and shelter you."

"I like the company of stone masons. We talk the same language. They appreciate good work. They are decent men. They learn their trade while they suckle their mother's milk."

Michelangelo sat with the men for some time and they talked of the qualities of marble from the quarries of Italy. "I once worked in a quarry as a young boy in Florence. When I grow weary of things, I return to the quarries. One should always return to the quarries. I hope you will not be lonely here, Andrea. You will miss the open spaces. Rome is a crowded place, teeming with evil. For every nun there is a thief. For every monk there is a black-hearted knave – and some of the knaves are artists." Clearly he did not like many of his colleagues.

"No. I will not be lonely. Giovanni and his family have promised to look after me."

Michelangelo invited them into the house. He showed them the vast plans which he had in mind. They were drawn on great sheets of paper, cartoons thrown carelessly about the place. "I need a patron. If I lived in Florence these drawings would have been executed in marble. They would have glorified the city. In Rome no one pays any heed to my work."

Andrea gazed in awe at the treasures so carelessly strewn about the place. "Will I ever possess such ability?" he asked.

"It is in the eye. Look carefully upon things. Follow line and mass. Sharpen your eyes. Most people are blind to the beauties about them," Michelangelo told him.

When they had visited the house, they returned to the yard. His father and Giovanni said goodbye to the boy. Andrea had carried his few belongings with him and Michelangleo directed him to a room in the rented house. When he returned to the yard, Michelangelo was busy working on a piece of sculpture. Andrea observed the intensity of his gaze.

Periodically somebody opened the wooden gate and entered the yard. They studied the sculptor at work. They never interrupted him.

Sometimes Michelangelo talked to them, never taking his eye off the marble figure.

"I prefer them to those in the Papal court," he told Andrea. "They are honest people. They breathe God's air. Their faults are not hidden. Observe them well. They are the substance of statues."

The boy had never seen anyone as clever as Michelangelo. The marble sang under his mallet and chisel. He moved with its grain. He never stopped his strokes until he had carved a definite line.

"Follow the grain to the end. If you leave off, it tells in the statue," he stated. "There is a shape or figure within the block. You must draw it out."

The sun grew hot. Michelangelo sat on the bench in the shade. He drank some water. Andrea looked at his hands. They were scored with old and new scars like those of the workers in the quarries.

He was a pleasant man to be with. He asked Andrea many questions concerning his family and made him feel at ease. He was about to begin work again when the gate opened and a gentleman entered. He was dressed in silk and wore an ornamental hat. At his side he carried a fine sword.

"Do you know Michelangelo?" he asked.

"The poor sculptor?" asked Michelangelo.

"I do not know whether he is poor or not," the gentleman said.

"Well I can assure you he is. And who seeks him?"

"The Pope."

"Perhaps Michelangelo has no wish to meet the Pope," the sculptor remarked.

"No one refuses the wish of the Pope," the gentleman replied haughtily.

"Then I will visit the Pope, for I am Michelangelo."

The gentleman was taken aback. He had expected the sculptor to be well-dressed and more presentable.

Michelangelo went indoors and when he reappeared he was dressed in good cotton clothes.

"Come with me, Andrea. Not many people meet the Pope on their second day in Rome," he laughed.

They followed the gentleman through the streets to the Vatican. They remained at some distance from him since he had no wish to be associated with them.

Finally they reached the Papal Palace. An old

friend, the architect Sangallo, was waiting for Michelangelo.

"The Pope has a commission for you. I have been talking to him. Follow me," he directed.

Andrea trailed behind the two men. His eyes were wide with excitement. He had never seen anything so beautiful in his life as the palace through which they now passed. In every corner and along every corridor stood marble and bronze statues. Great paintings hung on the walls. He did not have time to study them.

Eventually they arrived at a massive bronze door, panelled with sculptures. Two soldiers with drawn swords stood before it. They looked at Michelangelo and Andrea suspiciously.

Finally the great doors opened and they were invited to enter the Pope's chamber. Pope Julius sat on a golden throne, surrounded by cardinals and prelates. To Andrea he seemed very old and heavy-headed, and his face carried a long white beard. He was addressing someone. His voice was imperious and angry.

"Away you fool!" he roared dismissively. "Must I be always surrounded by incompetent people? Next!" he ordered. Some unfortunate fled from the Pope's presence.

Michelangelo, Sangallo and Andrea stood before the throne.They bowed and kissed the Pope's ring.

"You are Michelangelo?" the Pope asked.

"Yes."

"Who is with you?"

"An apprentice."

"Has he talent?"

"He is very talented."

Andrea looked at Pope Julius. His eyes seemed set far back in their sockets. They peered out from dark hollows. The boy was afraid of the pontiff.

"I have studied your Pietà. It is a fine piece of work. That is why you are here. I wish to commission my tomb; a large tomb for the centre of Saint Peter's. Prepare the plans and bring them to me. I want them as soon as possible. Good day."

That brought the brief audience to an end. They bowed and left the room.

"At last I have received a commission. I can promise you that there will be no tomb like it in Italy," Michelangelo told them.

"But when will it be finished?" Sangallo asked.

"I do not know. It will be vast and magnificent." His mind contemplated the great commission he had just received.

"You will spend your life carving such a monstrosity. It will be more than a tomb. It will be a palace for the dead," Sangallo commented.

"And to think that Christ lay in a borrowed tomb," Michelangelo commented. "As long as Julius can pay for his grand plans, I do not mind. If he wished me to carve a marble bath I would do it. If he wishes to lavish money on a tomb – I will carve a tomb."

That night they had a celebration in a tavern close to the yard. Everybody in the quarter was there, including the old man who sat on the marble form outside the gate. Michelangelo bought wine for everyone and even recited some poems he had written. He was in good form and told those present that he would carve them in marble and set them about the tomb.

"And where will you place me?" the fat old man asked.

"I will set you on a form just outside the tomb door," he replied.

"That would please me," the old man told him.

It was late when they reached the rented house. Andrea did not sleep very well that night. He recalled the vast palace he had visited and wondered how Michelangelo would set about designing the tomb. It seemed an impossible task. Then he fell asleep.

Next morning Michelangelo shook him awake.

"We must hurry. As soon as you have eaten your breakfast we will visit Saint Peter's basilica. I must seek a location for the tomb."

They hastened to the ancient church built by Constantine. Michelangelo studied the building very carefully. While he did so, Andrea examined the famous Pietà. He had never seen anything so beautiful in his life. Christ lay limply in the arms of his mother. On a band across her cloak Michelangelo had carved his name. He had been in his early twenties when he had carved the statue. The cascading drapery of the Madonna gave strength and unity to the masterpiece. It was one of the finest pieces of statuary ever created by man. It was at that moment that Andrea realised that he could never carve a piece of such quality. He turned around. Michelangelo was behind him. He was looking at his creation.

"I will never again chisel anything as fine," he said.

"You do not have to," the young boy said.

"Perhaps not as fine but more magnificent," the sculptor added.

Michelangelo studied the basilica again. It was falling to pieces. "A new church is necessary. Perhaps Sangallo will receive the commission. He is a decent man. But there is an architect in the city called Bramante, not a man I greatly like. I saw one of his buildings. He has true talent. He will challenge Sangallo . . . but let us forget the architects. We must hasten back to the yard. I have already decided upon a plan and I must set it down on paper."

Michelangelo spent a week working on the plan. He explained to Andrea the ideas and images which were forming in his mind. On several occasions they visited old Roman remains scattered about the city and examined them. Michelangelo's regard for the ancient masons was immense. "There is so much we can learn from them. They are our masters."

As he walked amongst the ancient ruins and sculptures of Rome, he taught Andrea many things about balance and harmony. "This tomb will be unique," he reflected as they rested after a day's labour.

"But will you have time to complete it?" Andrea asked.

"I have the skill and I can work rapidly on a project. It is money I need. The Pope has offered me nothing. Sometimes I feel I should return to the quarries or work with your uncle. At least I would be paid."

When the plans were ready, they had an audience with Julius II. The Pope laid out the drawings on a table and studied them carefully.

"This is excellent work. You must begin soon. You must acquire the most suitable blocks of marble."

"Marble costs money, your Holiness."

"Ah money. Yes, you will require money."

He called his secretary. "Give Michelangelo the sum of one thousand ducats. He will give you an account of his expenditure later. My secretary likes to keep a close eye on the manner in which money is spent."

The secretary brought them to his office. He counted out the ducats and put them in a leather purse. His face was thin and pinched and he had the sad countenance of a miser.

"Cheer up," Michelangelo told him. "It does not belong to you. It has been gathered from the poor of Christendom."

"The whole idea is an ill-conceived one. Ill-conceived. A smaller tomb would do," he remarked.

When they reached the street, Michelangelo handed Andrea a five ducat coin. "This is for you. You have earned it."

From his short acquaintance with Michelangelo, Andrea knew that the great sculptor set little value on money. On more than one occasion he had refused valuable commissions which would gratify some cardinal. He was interested only in creating great works of art.

"I will not sell my talents for their filthy money. I have pride in my craft."

They returned to the workshop where the design for the tomb had been created and where a small model had been made. About the tomb would be positioned thirty statues.

"We must now travel to Carrara and find the best blocks. I know what I need and your father will help me find them."

It took exactly a month to prepare for the journey. Andrea was excited by the fact that he would soon return to his village and visit his parents. Many nights he had cried on his pillow with loneliness. Rome was such a vast place and he was far away from his people.

"And on our way we shall visit many churches where you will find excellent works of art. I am tired of the city. I wish to be with my own kind – the masons and the sculptors and those who work in stone."

Michelangelo purchased two horses from a farmer. They were rough beasts, tired and overworked in the fields.

"He may know something of marble but he knows little of horses," the old man who sat on the bench close to the house told Andrea when he saw the two horses.

"They are sturdy and they will take us where we are going," Andrea replied. He always defended Michelangelo against caustic remarks, and the Romans had acid tongues.

Andrea packed the saddle bags with food and the drawings which he folded carefully.

It was an early summer morning when they left Rome. They travelled north. When they reached the crest of a hill they looked back. A fine mist softened the outlines of the buildings and the sun tinted the stones a rose colour.

"It looks beautiful," the boy said.

"Yes, on a morning such as this. But it has a rotten heart. It is an unfinished city. I would prefer to be in Florence working with the Medicis, but they have departed from the place."

They urged the horses forward and held to the coast. The road was good and on the left they could see the great waves, foam-tipped, rolling towards the shore. In the distance huge ships passed down the sea lanes on their way to Ostia, the Roman port. The plain through which they rode was green with young corn shoots. A light wind blew across the plain, rippling the surface. On the slopes of the hills were the vineyards. Men walked through the rows of vines, tending them as men had done for two thousand years. The scent of things growing was in the air. A few miles from Rome they stopped at a chapel and went inside. On the walls were several frescoes.

"They may not be as beautiful and complicated as those in Rome but they have a simplicity about them which I like. They were inspired by Fra Angelico, one of our greatest artists."

"Have you ever worked in frescoes or have you decorated a chapel wall?"

"No. And I don't intend to. I prefer to work in marble."

At a village they found an ancient statue discovered by a farmer in the ruins of an old pagan temple. Immediately Michelangelo began to examine it and ran his fingers along the carved lines. Then, with paper and charcoal, he quickly made a sketch of the statue.

"Observe it well. The sculptor knew what he was about. It is no mean work of art. No doubt the Pope or some cardinal will purchase it in Rome. At least it will be safe there. I once discovered an ancient statue used as a lintel in a barn."

Andrea had rarely seen Michelangelo in so good a mood. As they remounted their horses and moved through the plain, he began to sing songs he had learned in the quarry at Florence.

"They were composed to the stroke of a mallet," he explained.

They continued along the coast. Close to the shore fishermen were casting their nets and calling to one another. On their right the hills became more steep and beyond them stood the undulating Appenines, the very backbone of Italy, reaching up into the skies.

That night they found lodgings in a small fishing village. They ate a simple meal: fish from the sea and pasta. When they had finished, Michelangelo sketched the family. He drew them rapidly, catching each feature and character. Andrea observed him at work.

Michelangelo handed him a sheet of paper and some charcoal. "It is time for you to learn how to draw. You must catch the characteristics of people. Observe carefully. Sharpen your eyes."

Andrea worked on his drawings for an hour. Sometimes Michelangelo pointed out a mistake and gave him some instructions.

"That is excellent," Michelangelo said when he studied the finished work. "You have talent. Each day you must work on it. And keep your eye sharp for detail. Above all, your drawing must have life."

The people of the village were delighted with the drawings. They wished to purchase them but Michelangelo and Andrea gave them the drawings in exchange for the night's lodging. They were poor people, interested only in the gossip of the village and the harvest of the sea. They required little from life. They were simple religious people and they said goodbye to the two travellers with reluctance.

"Christ would be more at home in this village than in the Palace of the Pope in Rome," Michelangelo remarked as they moved down the coast.

They continued their journey towards Carrara, keeping as close to the sea as they could. In that way they avoided the haunts of the robbers in the hills. Finally, after many days, the quarries of Carrara came into view and soon afterwards Andrea's village. It was tucked neatly into the bowl of the mountain. The sun was shining on the cliffs of marble and they glowed with a golden light. Michelangelo studied them.

"Somewhere in those quarries lies the tomb of Julius II," he said. When they were half a mile from the village they noted people coming towards them.

Andrea urged his horse forward. When he was close to them he recognised his family and relations. He jumped from the horse and ran towards his father, who gathered him up in his arms.

That night they held a feast in the square. Everyone in the village was present. Michelangelo gave them all the news from Rome and they listened attentively while he told them of his many visits to the Pope. He told them also that he had brought money from Rome in order to purchase great blocks of marble.

"They have to be as white as snow and as fine as silk," he told them.

"We will take you to the ravines and valleys where you will find marble without fault or blemish, but it is difficult to obtain."

"I will go with you. I know these valleys well. I worked here for a time as a young man."

They spent the whole night talking about the qualities of marble and how it had been abused and used in various buildings. Their ancestors had worked in the quarries since Roman times and they were experts in their field. It was late when they retired to bed.

The very next morning they began the great work. Michelangelo was dressed like the other workers. He wore a loose shirt and trousers. They spent the day studying beds of marble. Finally Michelangelo found the marble he sought on a high cliff face. The work began.

It was a slow and tedious task and Michelangelo preferred to work with only a few helpers. Over the weeks and months great blocks of marble were cut from the cliff and slowly lowered to the quarry floor. They worked from morning till night cutting and finishing the great blocks and setting them in order.

They worked to a rhythm, breaking off in the middle of the day for a siesta. As the blocks were finished and marked, they were transported to the sea-shore. There they formed a wall on the sand. Every evening Michelangelo stood before the wall. He studied each block carefully, drawing out rough figures on them with charcoal. Sometimes he knocked on the blocks with a chisel and listened to the pure ring of healthy marble.

"It is has no fault," he would say to Andrea and the others who sometimes came with him. "It will make a fine statue. The statues are hidden within – it is my business to discover them."

It was tiring work which carried on through summer and autumn. The wind began to change. It blew down through the valleys sharp as a knife's edge. It cried on the crevices. The men hurried with their work. Finally the work was finished and Michelangelo paid the workers handsomely.

Now the marble had to be transported to Rome. The blocks were loaded onto rafts at the edge of the low tide. At full tide the rafts were floated to the barges and the blocks were winched on board. The bargemen raised their sails and began the slow journey southwards towards Rome. When the final block of marble had been safely placed on board, they held a farewell feast indoors.

It was time for Michelangelo and Andrea to return to Rome. Michelangelo had no wish to return to the city. He had noted a large crag of marble standing above the bay. It was visible from many miles down the coast and far out to sea. In its outline he had noted the figure of a colossus waiting to be freed. He would willingly have spent many years carving this vast shape. But his patron lived at Rome. He was a demanding pontiff and would brook no excuses.

It was a cold journey. The land was hardened by frost. The landscape was bare. The snows began to fall on the lower slopes of the Appenines. They set out for Rome in December.

CHAPTER 3

By the time they reached Rome, winter had set in. It was wet and cold. Grey clouds loomed above the city and the Tiber was in flood. The water was brown with sediment as it moved turbulently towards the sea. Michelangelo was anxious for the cargo of marble. Some of the blocks had arrived at the quays but others were still at sea. The great barges might not survive the storms. They were slow vessels, best suited to sluggish seas.

Michelangelo and Andrea arrived at the rented house. They were cold and miserable after the journey. The wind had cut them to the bone and even the woollen cloaks they wore did not keep the chill at bay. Michelangelo tore up several early drawings of the tomb, bundled them together and set them alight. Andrea placed some twigs about them. Then he piled dry branches and logs upon these and soon they had a warm fire blazing. The dry crackle of burning timber gave them some comfort. They stood near the fire until the chill had left their bodies.

The daughter of the old man who sat on the form outside the house brought them thick soup. She was a small plump lady and she gave them all the gossip of the quarter.

"And how is your father?" Michelangelo asked.

"Come December he retires to bed. He will rise again in February. However, it does not quieten his tongue or stifle his curiosity."

"I will visit him one of these days. I will tell him of my journey to the north. I have seen much that was of note and I can always stretch the stories."

"He would like that. He is very proud of his acquaintance with you. You should hear him at the tavern. He says that he suggests how you should draw your pictures and has given you advice on many matters."

Michelangelo began to laugh. "I like him. He is real. He has lived an interesting life. He has sailed the great seas. Tell him I shall call on him."

He took a bottle of wine from the dresser and handed it to the woman. "Tell him I received it from the Pope himself. It has been blessed three times and will cure all ailments."

"That will do him great good," she said, ladling out the soup into rough dishes.

They sat down and ate the thick soup and large chunks of bread. "This is what we needed, Andrea," Michelangelo said. "Heat for the body. It helps the mind to clear."

They had no sooner finished when a messenger arrived from Julius II. He wore a warm cloak of fur and heavy rings on his fingers.

"What news do you bring from the Vatican Palace?" Michelangelo asked.

"Julius intends to pull down the old basilica and erect one more magnificent and solid. It will be the glory of Christendom."

"Another tax on Christendom you mean," Michelangelo said.

"I would advise you to keep your thoughts to yourself," the messenger told him. "The Pope is the most powerful man in the world. One word from him and you would have to leave Rome; no more commissions, no more work."

The messenger was imperious and spoke with a falsetto voice. He gave the impression that each word uttered from his lips was precious.

"And where will I place his new tomb? I must know the proportions of this building. Have there been some initial plans set out that we can study?"

"I know nothing of these things. I merely came to tell you that a new basilica will be erected in place of the old. The Pope thought that you should know."

"The Pope did not mention money to you by any chance? I have spent many months in Carrara. I have used the thousand ducats to purchase marble. I am as poor as any beggar in Rome."

"I bring only a single message."

"Then bring a single message back to the Pope. Tell him both Michelangelo and his apprentice starve in cheap lodgings close to the Vatican Palace while he sups on rare foods."

"I bear messages from the Pope. I do not carry churlish words to him."

With that Michelangelo grew very angry. He grabbed one of his mallets and threw it at the messenger, who fled from the room.

"I hate this city. I would prefer to work in Florence. It is a civilized place where an artist is appreciated. Here he is an artisan. The Pope's tailor is more highly regarded."

"Soon the Pope will invite you to the palace and discuss the project with you," Andrea told him. He wished to temper his anger.

"One is not invited to visit the Pope. One is ordered to do so. All I wish is to carve marble. This is what I was born to do. This is the gift I received from God," he told Andrea.

"You must learn patience," Andrea told him. "You will get us both into trouble."

Michelangelo burst out laughing. "From the mouths of babes and sucklings you have perfected wisdom," he said, quoting the Bible.

There was a knock at the door. "Who is there?" Michelangelo called.

"Maria. We heard that you have returned from Carrara. I have brought you warm food."

"At last some good news. Two meals in an hour," Michelangelo said.

Andrea opened the door and let her in. She carried a warm vessel covered with a cotton cloth. She warmed the *cacciucco* or fish stew on the fire and then poured it onto plates.

"Mother felt that you would be perished after your journey. The weather is terrible. The men cannot work in the square."

"At least somebody cares for us in Rome. The Pope did not send us food."

While they ate, Maria tidied the rooms and placed some warm pans in the beds.

"My father said he will visit you this evening. Everybody is excited at the news that the Pope is going to erect a new chapel. They say that it will keep them employed for the next ten years."

"And who is the architect of this new church?"

"Bramante they say."

"Not Sangallo?"

"No, Bramante."

When Maria left, Michelangelo looked depressed. "This will break Sangallo's heart. He will be humiliated if he is not invited to design the new basilica. Perhaps it is not true. Rome feeds on rumours."

Giovanni arrived that evening. He sat before the fire and they drank mulled wine. They immediately began to talk of the new basilica commissioned by the Pope.

"And this new basilica which the Pope intends to build. Is it true that Bramante will receive the commission?" Michelangelo asked.

"It will be a open competition."

"Maria thinks Bramante has already received it."

"She listens to too much gossip. No. It will be an open competition. But I believe that Bramante could win. His style is in fashion."

"When will the results be announced?"

"In March."

The conversation changed. They began to talk of Carrara and the blocks of marble which were arriving at the port.

"I believe that most of the blocks have arrived at the docks by now," Giovanni said. "I have been to see them. Soon they will have to be removed. They are in a dangerous position. A quick flood and they could be swept to the bottom of the Tiber. It is a querulous type of river and not very dependable."

"Like the Pope himself," Michelangelo replied bitterly. "He has little regard for me. Others are wined and dined at the Vatican. They belong to the Papal court. They are the spoiled darlings of the city. They are praised and honoured."

"Among those who know, you are regarded as the greatest. Surely your Pietà is one of the finest works in the city. Your David in Florence will never be surpassed."

Giovanni could not really say what was on Michelangelo's mind. Michelangelo was careless in his demeanour. His beard was untidy, his appearance like that on a mendicant, and his clothes were rough and unfashionable. Besides, he was too direct in his words. It was not in his nature to flatter the Pope or the cardinals.

Their minds turned to more practical things.

"We must carry the blocks to a safe place in the city. We spent so long in the quarries picking the best blocks that it would be disastrous to lose them now. But it is what I would expect. Rome is an unlucky city for me."

"Then tomorrow I will organise the workers in the square," said Giovanni. "We will bring great carts to the docks and transport the blocks through the city."

"I cannot pay them at the moment," said Michelangelo.

"Pay them at another time. The Pope is bound to fill your purse with ducats."

"That will be the day," Michelangelo replied.

They talked late into the night. Then Giovanni said goodbye and set off to his quarter.

Next morning, as the thin winter light broke over the city, a dozen rough carts rolled out of the masons' quarters. They trundled through the streets in a long file. It was a cold morning and here and there ice lay on puddles. The garbage of the city was hardened by grey rime. The sharp wind penetrated their clothes and their breath formed plumes of frosted air.

At last they reached the docks. As they watched the barges, low in the water, weighed down by their inert cargo, they wondered if they could haul the great blocks onto secure ground. They constructed great tripods from firm poles of timber, secured pulleys beneath them and, working in unison, managed to lift the blocks onto planks and draw them across the cold morass to the bank. It was slow, tedious work. As soon as a block was loaded onto a cart, it was taken through the city. That evening a tenth of the blocks had been transpsorted to the Vatican. They placed them in the square in front of Saint Peter's. Next day they continued their work.

As Michelangelo watched the men haul the marble blocks through the streets, he felt pity for them. He immediately went to a friend in banking and borrowed money from him. That night he paid the workers and insisted they should eat the warm stew which Maria had prepared. It fortified them against the cold.

For eight days they worked at the arduous task. Soon they had to carry the blocks into the corridor leading to Castel Sant' Angelo. Michelangelo had picked some rooms here where he could work and where the Pope could visit him.

One night before their work had been completed, there was a heavy rainfall on the high hills. The Tiber flooded. Great swirling masses of water rushed between the ancient walled banks and rose above bank level. The Tiber rose about the great blocks, staining the white marble with river mud.

Michelangelo watched the waters rise above the blocks. Soon they were submerged.

Finally the water levels fell. The blocks were caked with slime and lodged in mud.

The workers set up the tripods and winches again and drew the final blocks to solid ground and raised them onto the carts. Then they were hauled through the streets to the Vatican.

When the work was finished, the masons stood with Michelangelo and studied the massive blocks of marble.

"Soon I will begin the great work. It will occupy me for ten years. When it is finished, it will be the greatest tomb ever created."

They did not doubt his words. They knew his worth. He was the greatest living sculptor in the world and perhaps of all ages.

Soon, however, this belief would be challenged. The challenge would come from the distant past.

It happened in January, on the Esquiline Hill. A Roman gardener was digging amongst his vines and clearing up the old leaves and dried twigs. Suddenly he came upon a niche on a slope. He had not noticed it before. Perhaps the rains had removed some earth from the slope. He cleared away the rubble and discovered a marble group in a niche. The figures were perfectly preserved.

He was aware that many ancient statues had been discovered in Rome. He had seen some of them. His eyes told him that this find was more precious than all the rest.

Immediately he sent a messenger to the Vatican with the news.

"We must get an expert to view this discovery," Pope Julius said. "Send for Sangallo."

As it happened, Michelangelo and Andrea were dining with Sangallo when the messenger arrived. He explained to them that a group of statues had been discovered. Immediately they set out for the Esquiline Hill.

They instantly recognised the group. It was the Laocoon described by Pliny the Elder fifteen hundred years earlier. Michelangelo could recite the exact passage describing the work. Standing in awe in front of the group, he quoted the relevant lines: "A work to be preferred to all that the arts of painting and sculpture have produced. Out of one block of stone the consummate artists Agesander, Polydorus, and Athenodorus of Rhodes made, after careful planning, Laocoon, his sons, and the snakes marvelloulsy entwining about them."

Michelangelo ran his fingers over the masterpiece which had been hidden for fifteen hundred years. "It is wonderful beyond words," he said. "Look at the chisel strokes and the polish. Look how well they understood the human form. There is much I can learn from this piece of work."

The piece was six feet in height. It was perfectly balanced and possessed immense energy. The eye never rested on any one part for long but travelled through all the linking lines.

The work was eventually moved to the Vatican. Many times during his life Michelangelo would return to this group and study the harmony and technique of the work.

Michelangelo now set about building a model. In the workshop, with the help of some carpenters, he supervised the construction of the tomb. When the proportions were correct he placed small columns of marble on the pedestals and niches where the statues would stand. In order to pay the carpenters and the masons, he had to raise the sum of a thousand ducats.

"This work will beggar me. Does the Pope not understand that I am not Midas!" he often cried in anguish.

Each evening after the day's work, Maria brought warm food to the workshop.

In March the results of the competition were announced. Bramante would build the new basilica on a scale never before attempted.

When Michelangelo first heard the news, his thoughts were for Sangallo. The old architect would be sorely disappointed. He depended for his livelihood on such commissions. Now that Bramante had been favoured by the Pope, several other commissions would flood into his office. Michelangelo's old friend could be left destitute.

"Let us examine the plans and the scales. I will hold my judgement until I have studied them carefully," he told Andrea.

They made their way to the Vatican. The plans were on display and beside them stood a large model. Michelangelo studied them thoughtfully. He was mute with admiration at the monumental idea.

"He is the best. Sangallo could not touch him," he said as they came away.

But his mind was disturbed by the plan. "They will destroy the old church and use the mosaics and tiles as foundations. Some of these are so beautiful that they cannot be replaced. These new architects believe that the past is of no value and has no beauty. Let them try and replace the mosaics and the pillars; then they would know."

Michelangelo visited the old church. He worried about the position of the tomb of Julius and about his Pietà.

When he asked some planners employed by

Bramante if part of the ancient basilica could be rescued, he was told that it was old and out of fashion.

"It will serve as a rubble foundation for the new basilica which will be built above the old foundations. These are the orders we have received from our master Bramante."

"He should not be called Bramante," Michelangelo said "but Ruinante." He walked away in disgust.

Quickly the phrase passed through Rome. It was believed that a great row was brewing between Bramante and Michelangelo. The architect had heard the remark and was furious. "What does a flat-nosed yokel know about architecture! He is a stone mason. It is the last and the least of the fine arts," Bramante retorted.

His reply was reported all over Rome. Michelangelo was furious.

"The Pietà and David were not created by a yokel," he cried. "I will challenge him to a duel."

"The only weapon he could use against me is a chisel and hammer," Bramante replied when he heard the remark.

One night as Michelangelo was returning home he was accosted by two men who suddenly appeared from a side street. They were Roman thugs and they held their daggers to his throat.

"Keep your mouth closed concerning the new basilica or we will cut your tongue out. Do you understand? Certain people in high places are greatly displeased with your remarks."

Michelangelo was terrified. He had no wish to turn up as a corpse in the Tiber. The men disappeared as quickly as they had appeared. Michelangelo was shaking with fear. He seemed to be surrounded by enemies. He was without money and it seemed that he would never begin the new monument. The Pope was ill-mannered and had not invited him for an audience.

"He must surely be aware of my poor condition," he said. "I stand ready to begin the work. Everything is meticulously planned and the Pope will not give me word to begin."

He could not work. Sometimes he took up his chisel to begin work on a statue but he left it down and went wandering through the streets. He recalled his youth in Florence when the Medici family had invited him to stay at their palace. There he had listened to the finest minds discuss the great topics of philosophy, art and politics. He had been well regarded in Florence. Lorenzo the Magnificent had been his patron. He could work in the sculptor's garden set out close to the palace. Those had been days of tremendous sweetness and joy.

In Rome he was neglected and poor. Sometimes he lacked intellectual company. There was no one with whom he could discuss his ideas. He dressed in poor clothes and was taken for a common peasant. He considered his future.

Michelangelo spent his evenings gazing at the great blocks of marble. They were like prisoners waiting to be released from white bondage.

Close by, the old basilica was being gutted. Great marble columns had been broken into blocks and mosaics chipped to pieces.

When he returned to his workshop he explained what had passed through his mind.

"This is a rotten city," he said. "I will shake its dust from my shoes."

"Arrange a meeting with the Pope. He has the

power to solve your problems," Maria told him.

"Is he interested in my problems? He is a warlord more interested in securing the Papal States than in the fortunes of a stone mason."

"He is the Pope. He has total power in the city," she replied. She had taken charge of his affairs and spoke to him as an equal.

"Very well. I will go visit the Pope," he told her.

"I will prepare your clothes. Some of them need stitching," Maria said. "You cannot stand in front of the Pope in peasant rags. You must have some regard for yourself."

"What would I do without both yourself and Andrea?" he asked.

"Very likely you would starve," she replied.

"Most likely," he added humbly.

Next morning, dressed in his finest clothes, he visited the Vatican Palace. Andrea accompanied him.

"Stand in line with the others," a footman told him. "The Pope has important visitors."

Michelangelo stood with the others. It was a humiliating experience.

The footman, filled with self-importance, called out various names in his official voice. Eventually he called out Michelangelo's name.

When he entered he knew that he would receive a cool reception. He should not have come. He should have taken his own advice and left the city. Pope Julius was in a vile mood.

"What do you want?" the Pope asked brusquely.

"Money," was the tart reply.

"And what of the tomb? Have you begun my tomb?"

"How can I begin without money?"

"You are bad-mannered."

"Possibly, but I am also poor."

The Pope's countenance turned purple with anger. He raised his stick and shook it in Michelangelo's face. "I have never met such a strong-headed person in my life. I order you to begin the tomb. Return in a week and I shall discuss the matter with you. Be on your way. I have more important business to attend to. I need men who can cast weapons of war, not sculptors. The very existence of the Papal States are in the balance."

Michelangelo left the presence of the Pope, followed by Andrea.

"That Pope has my heart broken," he said. "He was in a terrible mood. I thought he might have a seizure."

"He's too tough for that," Andrea said.

They walked along the banks of the Tiber. For a long while Michelangelo did not speak.

Suddenly he said, "I know what I will do! I will leave the city. I will return to Florence. We must make preparations. You will come with me. You are the only witness I have to all the misfortune which has befallen me. When will I do what I do best – carve marble?"

That night he sat down and wrote a letter to the Pope listing his complaints. He spent a long time over its composition. It was well written and to the point. He read it out loud for Maria and Andrea.

"That should settle the question once and for all. I'm done with this place."

It would be delivered to the Pope when Michelangelo was well free of the city.

Andrea prepared the animals for the flight from Rome. The old man, who had recovered from his winter illness, watched the young boy make ready the horses.

"As I said before, he may be a good sculptor but he is a poor judge of a horse. I wouldn't bet my life on them. Are you going far?"

"Not very far," Andrea replied.

"Well, from the preparations I would say that you intend to go a great distance. I believe that he is not getting on well with the Pope?"

"Who told you that?"

"I hear things."

"It's true. Things have been going badly between them."

"He is a powerful man to take on the Pope and he with the keys of heaven in his pocket. If he has a bottle of wine blessed three times by the Pope and is not in need of it, he can give it to me. I feel ten times younger since I drank the last one."

Andrea went indoors and brought out two bottles of wine.

"You are in luck," he said. "These bottles have been blessed four times by the Pope together with five cardinals."

"I am most obliged. I will treasure them," the old man said.

In the meantime, Maria was making the final preparations for departure. She insisted that they take warm clothes and plenty of food.

"I am sure you will be back," she said. "So I will keep the place well aired."

"I will never come back unless I come back in chains," Michelangelo said.

Before he left he took several priceless sketches and threw them in the fire.

"If he wishes to draw his tomb, then he can draw it himself," Michelangelo said.

"That was a foolish thing to have done," Maria told

him. "These drawings are of great value."

"I don't care," Michelangelo replied tartly.

"No wonder the Pope cannot get along with you. You have too fiery a temper."

Michelangelo was in one of his bad moods and would not listen to reason.

"Let us be one our way," he ordered.

Michelangelo and Andrea mounted their horses.

The old man was sitting on his form. "Blessings upon you," he said.

"Thanks," said Michelangelo. "One honourable Roman has turned up to wish us good luck."

They ordered their horses forward through the narrow streets, travelling quickly across country like fleeing criminals. They stopped each night at some obscure inn along the way. Sometimes they slept in barns. They were certain that they would soon be outside the power of Julius II.

Then one morning as they were saddling their horses they noticed a dust cloud in the valley below them. They recognised the Papal riders with their escutcheons and flags.

They were about to mount their horses and flee when the horsemen bore down upon them and cast a circle about them.

"Where are you bound?" the leader asked.

"We travel to Florence," Michelangelo replied.

"You are requested in Rome by the Pope. It is my business to see you return."

There was a heavy threat in his voice.

"As prisoners?"

"If necessary. I think it would be better if you came quietly."

"I will continue to Florence. I am finished with Rome," Michelangelo told the leader.

One of the soldiers took out his sword. “Place your sword in its scabbard. I was ordered not to harm him. He will return eventually. The Pope’s power is wide. The Pope will be very angry,” the leader said.

“Well tell him that Michelangelo is angry at the neglect he has received at his hands.”

The captain turned his horse and with that they disappeared as swiftly as they had appeared. The dust swirled about them as they rode back towards Rome.

“Were you afraid?” Andrea asked.

“Of course I was,” Michelangelo replied.

They continued their journey. Finally they reached the hills above Florence. They looked down at the red-roofed houses: the towers and the great dome by Brunelleschi.

“There is no place compared to it on earth. Even the air is fresh and sweet. Here I learned my craft. It was here I first felt the attraction of marble.”

There was joy in his heart and his voice was filled with enthusiasm for the city of Florence. “I shall be free here. I shall be free from that Pope who ill used me.”

But Andrea had learned much in Rome. He knew that if the Pope required a statue, he would have a statue. Michelangelo would never be free from his power.

They urged their horses downhill towards the enchanted city.

CHAPTER 4

Now that Michelangelo had departed from Rome, Bramante was all powerful. Everyone spoke of him. He was about to undertake the construction of the greatest church in Christendom.

"He tried to destroy my reputation," Bramante often said of Michelangelo to his friends. "Now he is yesterday's man. Who will want to employ a stone mason who has insulted the Pope?"

"Does the Pope's power stretch as far as Florence?" a young admirer asked.

"The Pope's power stretches to the very ends of the earth. Michelangelo is *persona non grata.*"

They laughed at the misfortune that had befallen the sculptor. Many others were delighted that Michelangelo had left Rome. He lacked dignity in appearance and behaviour. He looked more like a peasant than a sculptor. His crooked nose, the result of a fight, did not help his image.

There were, however, some who regretted his departure. They knew that he could change the appearance of the Vatican if he were given a free hand. His artistic talents were boundless.

But Pope Julius had not forgotten Michelangelo. For the moment he had to put him to the back of his mind. He knew the value of the man and he would put his talents to some use. He had lost interest in the tomb. The design and execution of Saint Peter's new basilica was more important. He was pleased with the new design. It was serious and dignified and would cost a great deal. He was also engaged in preparations for war and was gathering an army about him.

The Pope revelled in the active life. He understood the ways of war and had the mind and tongue of a soldier. Julius had many political issues to settle. He was surrounded by enemies who would move upon the Papal States and wrest them from him. But he would not yield an acre. He would move against his enemies and destroy them with his spiritual and military power. If Julius could not beat them in the field, he could damn them to hell.

Venice, built on shallow mudflats and timber piles, was an old enemy. The Venetians were wealthy. Their great fleets had brought them limitless wealth and their palaces set along the canals were beautiful to behold. The Venetians were cunning and treacherous.

The Pope gathered his captains. They stood about a map of Italy and studied it carefully.

"I have spies placed all over Italy; in convents, seminaries and in monasteries. I have men positioned in all the courts. I know what my enemies think. They believe that I am too old to wage war at sixty-three. But I will teach them a lesson, one they will never forget," he said in a rough voice.

One of his captains explained the military position to those gathered about the great map. "With our present force we can move against Perugia and Bologna. They are not prepared to meet us."

The Pope went over the details of the campaign with his captains. He wished to know how many horsemen they possessed and how many cannons they could carry into the field. He also inquired after the health of the soldiers.

"Ensure that the troops are well fed and well clothed. No army should go into battle ill fed or ill clothed. It brings on fever and dysentery. Place them all on a war alert." Then he dismissed them.

He stood above the map and considered the moves he would make against his enemies as a chess player considers the best moves against an opponent.

The door swung open and Bramante appeared. He carried with him a sheaf of plans which he set out on the table over the map of Italy.

The Pope studied the plans for the new basilica. "And where will my tomb be positioned?" he asked.

"I did not draw it into any of the plans."

"Why?"

"I am superstitious concerning such a tomb. It could bring you bad luck. The sooner it is finished, the sooner you will lie in it."

The statement shook the Pope. He considered the idea. Perhaps the architect was right. He could be drawing death upon him.

"And what task will I set for that renegade Michelangelo? No doubt he thinks that he is safe from my anger in Florence. He has insulted me you know. Have you any suggestions?"

"Yes," said Bramante with a smile on his face.

"Tell me quickly," the Pope urged.

"Commission him to paint the Sistine Chapel," he suggested.

The Pope burst out laughing. "Paint that ugly barn of a building? There is neither shape nor make to it."

"I know."

"But he is not a painter."

"I know. But you are master of the world. He will have to obey you."

"Paint the Sistine Chapel," the Pope said again. "That would be a joke. That would teach the blackguard a lesson. I believe that you have solved my problem. I will give him the ugly building to paint."

The Pope laughed again, this time joined by Bramante.

"I will write a stiff letter to him."

Everybody in Rome soon heard the news. Like the Pope they laughed at the idea. Bramante had made a fool of Michelangelo.

Soon the news reached Florence. Michelangelo was furious when he heard the suggestion.

"I am not a painter. I have no experience of roof and wall paintings. That is for the fresco workers. Only Leonardo da Vinci or Raphael is capable of such work."

Anger raged through his being. He left the city and went to work in the quarries close to Florence where he had begun to carve marble for the first time. He worked from morning until night with the quarry men, cutting large blocks of marble from the quarry face, sleeping at night in a small attic.

Andrea worked with him in the quarry. Then one day Michelangelo presented him with a square of marble. "This heavy work is too much for you. Take this slim piece of marble and carve a Madonna from it. It is time you created your own work."

Andrea, who had drawn several Madonnas on his travels, took the studies from his satchel and began his work. Every evening he showed Michelangelo what he had done.

"Good. Be friendly towards the grain. Draw out the figure. Seek the delicate outline. Even the young face of the Virgin was visited by sorrow."

Andrea worked on the marble with the fine chisels his father had made for him. He recalled the face of a young woman in Rome who had lost her child. He tried to impose this sorrow upon his Madonna.

"Each day you improve," Michelangelo told him as they sat in the evening sun outside the house where they had lodgings.

"Will you ever return to Rome?" Andrea asked him.

"I would prefer to live here. But the power of the Pope extends into every corner of Europe. I cannot obtain a commission in Florence. Everyone finds some reason to refuse me. The real reason is of course that they are afraid of the Pope."

"Could you paint the Sistine Chapel?"

"Perhaps. I would have to study the place and find experts in the techniques of fresco. But I am a sculptor. When will the Pope realise that simple fact?"

They spent many days in the village above Florence. Then they returned to the city. A letter from the Pope awaited him. He read it carefully. It was an invitation to go to Rome.

"No. I will not go. I believe that the Sultan of Turkey requires a bridge builder, so the Franciscan Fathers say. They have extended an invitation to me to visit Turkey. It would be interesting to build a bridge which would join two continents."

"You would work for a Moslem Prince?"

"Indeed I would. He is probably better bred than the Pope. He would pay me well and extend hospitality towards me."

Michelangelo remained in Florence. The Pope was now engaged in war and Michelangelo felt that Julius II had forgotten about his very existence. But he was wrong.

In May the Pope left Rome with an army. He moved on Perugia and beat the state into submission. Then he moved quickly across the Appenines. He marched into Bologna.

While the war was waging, Michelangelo began to work on a statue of Saint Matthew. It was the first time that Andrea had seen Michelangelo at work on an original block of marble. The figure of the apostle began to emerge from the statue like a body submerged in water that is slowly pulled to the surface. The lines of the body, the tension and torment of the face appeared ever so slowly. Andrea knew that the face carried all the pain and torture which the sculptor was suffering at that moment. He was freeing the figure from the block of marble and at the same time was easing the pain out his mind.

While he worked on the statue further messengers arrived from Pope Julius. Michelangelo told them that he would soon make a journey to Turkey and serve the Sultan. The Sultan would pay him well and show him some respect. Why should he remain in Italy when he could not receive a decent commission?

News of the correspondence between the Pope and the sculptor spread throughout the city.

While Michelangelo worked on his statue of Saint Matthew, Andrea continued to work on his Madonna.

Every morning after breakfast Andrea left the house in which they stayed and explored the city. It was far more beautiful and intimate than Rome. Everywhere there was some work of art to study; the architecture of Brunelleschi, the paintings of Masaccio, Fra Angelico, Paolo Uccello, Filippo Lippi, Botticelli and many others.

In the centre of the city was the magnificent tower by Giotto. It was tall, white and finely finished. The great bronze doors carried some of the finest panelling ever cast in Italy.

Andrea carried his sketchbook with him. Frequently he sat before some masterpiece and began to make rapid sketches of what he saw. Soon he began to grasp the order and balance of the works of art. He was beginning to understand the spirit of the Renaissance.

Each evening he showed his work to the master. Michelangelo corrected his mistakes with a quick sweep of a charcoal stub.

"You must also study people. Sit on the Ponte Vecchio and observe the multitudes that move across it. Study the expressions on the faces – everything is written into the face – time is the sculptor."

After that, Andrea often sat on the Ponte Vecchio which spanned the River Arno and watched the crowd.

In Florence Andrea received his education. It was there that he finished his Madonna which he sold for five ducats. He showed the fee to Michelangelo.

"Well done. You have begun your career. You have earned your first money."

Michelangelo was happy in Florence. He renewed acquaintance with many of his friends. The artists were friendlier and less jealous than they were in

Rome. He thought that this pleasant life would continue – but it was not to be.

One day a Papal letter arrived from Bologna. Julius II wished to see him. News of the letter passed through Florence.

"He must meet the Pope's request," they argued. "He could bring the wrath of the pontiff upon the city. We are ill prepared to meet his army in battle."

Now the city turned against Michelangelo. They refused to speak to him and many turned their back upon him.

"Soon they will stone me," he told Andrea. "The Pope has won again. We must set off for Bologna."

They left for Bologna in November. The wind was bitter and cut them to the bone. As they passed higher into the mountains it grew colder and snow began to fall. Finally they reached the city. It was filled with soldiers. Mass was in progress when they entered the chapel of San Petronio. They stood with the congregation. They were quickly noticed by one of the Pope's servants. He immediately approached them.

"The Pope is at the Palazzo de Sedici. We have been instructed to bring you into his presence immediately on your arrival. Follow me."

They followed the servant.

"Things look serious," Michelangelo said to Andrea as they passed through the throngs of soldiers.

"The city looks like a military camp," Andrea remarked.

"Not a place in which to create great art," Michelangelo replied.

They reached the palace. It was a hive of activity. Cardinals, prelates and soldiers moved rapidly through the corridors and great rooms.

They entered the dining-room. It was a splendid place. The rarest fruit lay in pyramids on silver bowls and the finest meat was set out on huge platters. The conversation was loud and confused. Julius II sat at the head of the table.

When Michelangelo and Andrea entered the room the conversation ceased. The Pope and the sculptor stared at each other.

"I have had to come on a long journey to meet you," Julius said.

"You ill used me in Rome. I was thrown out of the Vatican Palace by arrogant servants."

Men stared with open mouths at Michelangelo and the Pope. A bishop spoke.

"You cannot speak in such a manner to the Pope. You are but a sculptor."

The Pope hit the table with his fist. He spoke to the bishop. There was anger in his voice. "You cannot speak in that fashion to such a great artist. You have bad manners." He called his servants. "Throw the bishop out," he said.

Immediately the servants grabbed the bishop. They lifted him from his chair and carried him to the door. Unceremoniously they threw him out into the gutter.

"I can always replace a bishop. It is different with a sculptor. Come here," Pope Julius demanded.

Michelangelo made his way up the great hall. All eyes were upon him. He knelt down.

"You are forgiven. Do not leave Bologna. I have work for you here. Tomorrow visit me at my camp. There we can discuss our business."

Outside the air was sharp. Great flakes of snow were falling on the square and on the domes and rooftops of the city. The soldiers had built bonfires against the cold and were gathered about them. Michelangelo and Andrea passed through the city now muted by snow.

"What plan has he in mind for you?" Andrea asked.

"Only God and the Pope knows. Tomorrow we will find out."

It was almost impossible to find lodgings for the night. Finally a butcher hired them a loft in his barn. It was occupied by soldiers, who spent the night drinking and swearing. It was a place without comfort. They drew their cloaks about them and tried to sleep. They were woken by the sound of drum-beats. The soldiers stirred drunkenly.

"A cold day. Will the Pope's blessings stave off the blows of our enemies?" one soldier asked.

"John from Lombardy went into battle carrying sacred images. His head was split," came the reply.

"You have little reverence," his companion said.

"I pray, not loud, but I pray," the other replied.

"It is foul weather for war."

"Any day one goes into battle is a foul day."

They continued to talk as they fastened their swordbelts and drew on leather gloves. The loft was cold and their breath was grey. Climbing down the rough ladder and breaking the ice on a barrel, they washed the nightsleep from their eyes. Michelangelo and Andrea followed them. Then they went in search of food. Like every other commodity in Bologna it had doubled in price. They found a merchant who sold salami and made coarse sandwiches. They washed the food down with cold water.

Then they set out for the military camp, following a drummer and a group of soldiers. Finally they reached the camp. The ground was churned up and muddy. Men cursed their horses and each other as they waded knee deep in mud. Coloured tents carrying escutcheons and pennants stood in a sea of mud. In the centre of the confusion stood Julius II, a great fur robe about him. He was with his captains and soldiers discussing the strategy of the day. His was the rough language of the field camp and the battlefield and the captains and soldiers enjoyed his gruff exchanges with them.

"Ah, you have come, Michelangelo. I thought perhaps you might flee from me again. Come to my camp, both of you. We shall drink mulled wine."

The pontiff strode ahead of them. Despite his age, he was filled with energy and enthusiasm.

"He should have been a general," Michelangelo said.

They came to a great tent bearing the Papal escutcheons. The guards drew the flaps aside and they entered. It was a warm comfortable place heated by a portable stove. They sat down and wine was set before them. It was warm and perfumed.

"Let us get directly to business. Soon I will have to move to the front and lead my army. I wish to have my figure cast in bronze. I want it done quickly. I fear that I may die in the field of battle and no decent memorial remains to me."

"There are others better qualified for the task. I am a sculptor."

The Pope grew angry. He placed his hand on his sword hilt. "You are not qualified to build bridges, yet you would do so for the Sultan. I am tired of your refusals, your continual complaints. Your pontiff has given you a command. Do you understand?" he bellowed.

"Yes, your Holiness."

"Good, that is settled. I have to go to battle and

you have to prepare your work."

"Yes, your Holiness."

"I'm sure you will need money. You always complain about money."

"That is correct. The prices have doubled in the city due to this war. Last night we slept on hay."

"So did Christ."

Julius handed him a bag of gold. With that the Pope dismissed him.

"Is there no end to trouble? I work in marble. I have never cast anything in bronze. Now I have to learn the whole technique in a matter of weeks. I am a slave to this Pope."

They passed through the battlefield. Drums were sounding soldiers into formation and trumpets calling them forward. The camp was falling into battle order. That night many of the young men would be dead.

"I have no taste for war. Let us hasten away from this place before the Pope orders me into battle. We must find a proper place to work."

They spent the day searching for good quarters. Finally they discovered what they needed in a side street, away from the military bustle of the city. It was a spacious house with a large walled garden.

"I am pleased with the work space. We have heat and we have food. Now I must acquaint myself with the art of casting bronze. I have friends in Florence who are skilled in such matters. I will seek their help," Michelangelo said when they had settled in.

He was pleased in a sense that he had found work to do. He wrote a letter to some bronze workers. It carried the Papal seal. "That should frighten and impress them," he said as he dispatched the letter.

The bronze workers came immediately to Bologna. They sat down and explained to him the difficult task of casting bronze. Quickly Michelangelo learned their techniques. They bought wax, moulding clay and bricks. These were carried to the yard in preparation for the casting. Michelangelo was generous to them. He gave them money to buy food and clothing. Soon, however, they began to complain.

"Things are overpriced in Bologna. War makes want and want sends prices soaring. We cannot purchase wine or food."

Michelangelo set off to meet the Pope. The Pope was in a bilious mood. "What brings you here?"

"Money."

"Why?"

"In order to begin the memorial statue."

"Did I not supply you with an ample sum?"

"I brought experts in from Florence. They have expensive tastes."

"I have to feed an army. War consumes money." He called his secretary, who handed him a hundred ducats. "Now be careful with the money."

Michelangelo returned to the house and began work on the statue. He had done initial studies of the Pope and he worked from these. He quickly shaped the figure in clay. He worked rapidly, gouging out the shape of the face and the hollow eyes. Soon a small model was almost complete. The Pope came to visit him. He studied the clay model. "You have placed nothing in my hand," he said.

"I intended to have you holding a book."

"A sword would be more suitable. I have no great aptitude or time for learning. Yes, place a sword in my hand."

Michelangelo continued with the model. He had now to make it life size and this took considerable time, building the skeleton of wire and timber and moulding the clay about it.

The winter passed and spring arrived. It brought not only an early leaf to the vine but also the plague. Each morning the carts passed through the city gathering the dead. Every day the funeral bell tolled dully. Each evening fires were lit to ward off the plague.

Michelangelo and Andrea worked on the monumental figure in the garden helped by two experts in casting. But one night the experts fled the city. They had seen the dreadful effects of the plague and had no wish to die.

"I believe that you should also leave," Michelangelo said. "You are too young to die. Return to your parents."

"No, I will remain with you. I came here to learn the secrets of the human figure and I could have no greater master."

"You have a lion's heart. Let us continue this burdensome statue. Soon it will be ready for the furnace."

The Pope visited Michelangelo before he left the city. He was pleased with the figure. "It is time to cast it," he told him and left.

Michelangelo had no experience in casting statues. He found someone who was an expert in the field. A mould was taken of the statue. Wax was set within the mould. The mould was surrounded by plaster which set to the shape. The wax was melted and drawn away. Then a wall of brick was built about the rough plaster and the bronze poured. The first casting failed. They began the task again. After three weeks they removed the bricks and the plaster. The metals had fused and the rough bronze statue stood before them.

"We have succeeded," said Michelangelo with

pleasure. "Now we must polish the bronze until it sparkles."

They began the work of polishing the rough bronze. It was painful work which tore their hands. Their mouths were filled with the sour taste of metal. Finally it began to take on a bright patina. They studied the work with critical eyes.

"I could have done no better," Michelangelo told Andrea. "But why must I do work which goes against the grain of my talent?"

They began to grow weary of the tedious work. One day it was finished. The massive statue was placed before the church of San Petronio in February 1508.

"I am now free from this monstrous task," Michelangelo told Andrea. "Let us pack our bags and go."

In March they left the city. They did not look back at the city scape with its churches and towers, but set their sights on Michelangelo's beloved city of Florence.

Chapter 5

They were standing on the Ponte Vecchio. "This is the most wonderful of cities," Michelangelo remarked. "Florence has style. The breath of freedom blows through its streets."

A great crowd moved across the bridge. On either side stood shops stocked with innumerable articles. Beneath the bridge the River Arno, muddied with silt, made its way sluggishly towards the sea. Everybody knew Michelangelo and appreciated his worth. He had carved the most impressive statue in Italy. The statue of David, tall as a two-storied building, had become the symbol of the city.

"You were right," Andrea told him. "In every quarter of the city, in every convent, monastery and chapel is some work of great art."

"This is an ordered place thanks to the Medici family. Lorenzo the Magnificent was a true humanist.

Everything interested him. Rome is a city of confusion. I detest the place. I hope that I shall never have to return. It is unfinished, like a half-plucked goose."

"Do not let the Pope hear you talk in that manner."

"I will be free to talk. I am not a toady like Bramante and Raphael."

They continued their walk across the city. Michelangelo was in a happy mood. He had finished his work in Bologna and was independent of the Pope. They encountered the great artist Sandro Botticelli in the Piazza della Signoria. His father had been a tanner and he had received the name Botticelli or Little Barrel as a nickname when he was very young. He was sitting on a marble seat. The famous painter was old and he looked emaciated and hungry.

"How is life treating you?" Michelangelo asked him.

"It treats me badly. I can no longer work. My hands tremble when I hold a brush. They are worthless now."

Andrea gazed in awe at the old man with the trembling hands. He had painted the most exquisite pictures he had ever seen: Primavera and The birth of Venus. No painter in Italy had ever accomplished such work.

"The heart went out of the city when they expelled the Medici family. They understood works of art. It was the golden age of the city. I remember Fra Filippo Lippi. I was his apprentice for a while. Then I worked for Andrea del Verrocchio. You name them, I knew them. Leonardo da Vinci was here during those times. He had a restless mind, that man. He never finished anything properly. He thought we could fly. Well, I tell you, Michelangelo, if God wished us to fly he would have given us wings." Botticelli began to shake with laughter. He exposed his black and rotting teeth.

He flapped his hands in imitation of bird flight.

"I have studied your paintings," Andrea said. "They are filled with delight and glorious colours – particularly the Primavera and The birth of Venus."

"It was spring in my heart then, son. There was so much more I could have achieved. But along came Savonarola. The monk had a gloomy mind. There was no delight in it. I saw the finest of art burnt in the square at his instruction. He took delight in nothing. He was joyless. I was here the day they hanged and burned him."

His mind turned gloomy when he thought of those dark times. He looked at the boy.

"Are you an artist?"

"He is," Michelangelo told him. "He has already sold his first marble."

"And did he get paid?" asked Botticelli.

"He did."

The old man turned to Andrea. "Let me give you some advice. Hold on to your money or you will end up like myself and Michelangelo. We haven't a ducat to call our own." And with that he began to laugh again.

The sun was now high in the sky and beating down on the square.

"Will you come home with us?" Michelangelo asked. "I have purchased marzolini cheese and white wine."

The old man's eyes brightened. "I will join you. It is too warm and the midday sun dries the body." He rose stiffly from his seat and walked with them.

They walked through the city which was very familiar to them. It was full of precious memories. Frequently they stood before some building or statue. They studied its quality and spoke familiarly about everything. They had helped to beautify the city and were proud of their achievement.

"The artist will be long remembered when he is dead and gone. Not so the politician or the priest," Andrea told them.

"Its a pity that they don't have more respect for them while they live," Botticelli said.

"And pay them their just rewards," Michelangelo added.

"And treat them better than they do. I believe that the Pope has greatly abused you, Michelangelo."

"Don't mention the Pope. I am well and truly free of him. I almost starved in Rome. I have lost precious years. Outside the Vatican are the finest blocks of marble you have ever seen and I will never get the chance to sculpt them."

"It's a wicked city," Botticelli remarked.

"Don't mention the place."

They turned their attention to other subjects as they walked slowly through the streets. Every street held a memory for the artist. Eventually they reached the house near Santa Croce. There they sat in the garden, drank the wine and ate the cheese.

"This is a fine life," Sandro Botticelli said when he had eaten his fill. "I can't chew meat anymore. But a good cheese always gives me heart."

There was a strong scent from the flowers and the bees were busy gathering nectar. The sun was moving across the sky and the garden was filled with shadows. Peace reigned in the walled place.

"I once planned to buy a farm in the hills above Florence," Botticelli said.

"But you are not a farmer," Michelangelo told him.

"I would have learned the noble art of agriculture and I would have built a garden with running water. I would sit in the shade and look down upon Florence with its towers and roofs and the huge dome of the Cathedral of Santa Maria del Fiore constructed by the great Brunelleschi. And I would paint beautiful pictures."

"What happened?"

"The monk Savonarola happened. My mind went dark. It has become bright again but my hands are of no use." Again he held up his hands which trembled involuntarily.

The conversation was pleasant in this cool place. Suddenly there was a commotion within the house. A cardinal appeared in the garden followed by his servant. He carried a letter which he pushed in Michelangelo's face.

"Read this," he said roughly.

"You may have power but you lack manners," Michelangelo told him. "You have disturbed the peace of this place." He took the letter and left it aside. "I will read it later. Can you not see that I am in the company of fellow artists?"

"Read it. It comes directly from the Pope," the cardinal ordered.

"He can wait. I have had to wait for him in Rome. He humiliated me. He beggared me. If he requires a reply, I will send him a reply."

"That's the way to talk to them. They are an arrogant lot!" Botticelli called out. He was slightly drunk.

"Who is this toothless fool?" the cardinal asked.

"He is Sandro Botticelli. His paintings hang in the Sistine Chapel."

"And you will soon have a ceiling all to yourself above them," the cardinal said with a smile on his face.

Michelangelo tore the letter open. He read its

contents. It was an invitation to Rome.

"It says nothing here concerning the Sistine Chapel."

"There is a rumour in Rome that the Pope is going to give you a commission to paint the ceiling."

"This is the work of Bramante and Raphael. They have the Pope's ear. They are schemers. They place obstacles in my way. I will never paint the ceiling of the Sistine Chapel. I must carve marble."

The cardinal was unmoved. "The Pope requires an answer. I will return tomorrow for a reply." With that he gathered his robes about him and left the garden.

"I remember the time I spent in that chapel. I was there in the year '81 or was it '82? My head is addled. That's not a chapel. It was designed as a fortress. I did three paintings for the Pope. I tell you I wouldn't like to have to paint that ceiling. It's crooked. There is neither shape nor make to it."

"I know. I visited it. Nobody could undertake such work. It is a Herculean task."

"Well, Hercules wouldn't do it because Hercules was a pagan," Sandro Botticelli said.

"What answer will you give the Pope?" Andrea asked.

"I will have to return to Rome. The Pope is too powerful. His power stretches to this city. But I cannot paint frescoes."

"Get advice. There are lots of fresco painters in Florence who need the work. Talk to them. Bring them to Rome," Botticelli advised.

"They may be able to fresco walls. But can they fresco ceilings?" Michelangelo asked.

"A ceiling is a bent wall upside down," Sandro Botticelli replied, simplifying the whole problem.

Michelangelo began to laugh.

Later Sandro Botticelli spoke knowledgeably about frescoes. Michelangelo listened intently to his words.

"When you are painting frescoes you have to be fast. You have to be careful with the mixtures for the plaster. Never have it too wet or too dry. Prepare a day's work in advance."

"Do you realise how vast that ceiling is?"

"Of course I do. Didn't I work there in '82 or was it '83? I'm confused. I was delighted to return to this city. The air is sweet here."

Darkness fell. They carried lanterns into the garden and talked in the soft, half-shadowy light.

"If I were young I would go with you. Look at my hands. They shake. I can no longer work." He began to weep quietly. He was tired. Michelangelo put a hand on his shoulder.

"You are the best. You have been given a divine gift and you have used it well."

Botticelli looked at Michelangelo. "Do you think so? Do you really think so? You are not saying that to please me?"

"As an artist I tell you no lie."

"From you that is the greatest compliment any artist can receive. I have prayed before your Pietà. I am not a great prayer but I prayed before it. It softens the heart – not many statues soften the heart."

Botticelli was too drunk to walk to his bed. Michelangelo lifted him from his seat and carried him into the house as if he were a baby. It was warm in the room and he set him down on the bed. Soon the old painter was fast asleep.

Michelangelo said good night to Andrea and returned to the garden. He put out the lantern lights and gazed at the sky which arched above him. He had much to think about. Perhaps the cardinal had been wrong. The letter did not mention the Sistine ceiling, and rumours could never be believed. Once again he looked at the ceiling of stars above him. The night sky was a great vault. His imagination started to fill up the vault with human figures. It was almost daybreak when he left the garden. There was a silver light in the east and the air was fresh and perfumed. He had made up his mind. He would make the journey to Rome. He sat down and wrote a letter of acceptance. It was ready for the cardinal when he arrived.

A few days later Michelangelo and Andrea set off for Rome. They returned to the house they had occupied before their departure. The old man was sitting on the form.

"The blessed bottles of wine worked wonders," he said.

"Good," Michelangelo replied.

"I missed you. Did you travel far?"

"We were in Florence and Bologna."

"Were you in the war?"

"No, but we were on the edge of it."

"Did the fever get you?"

"No."

"You're a hardy man, a hardy man."

They went indoors. "At least some things never change," Michelangelo told Andrea.

The next day they set out for the Vatican palace. "The Pope will now see you," a servant said, addressing them in a superior voice. They had been waiting for two hours in a long corridor with an arched ceiling. Michelangelo spent his time studying it, setting out a scheme of frescoes on its white surface.

They passed between tall bronze doors. The room was filled with clerics and cardinals and was scented with perfumes.

"Ah, my old friend and enemy," the Pope said when he saw the sculptor.

"Your servant always," Michelangelo replied.

"I note that you have become humble and obedient. This is certainly a change. They tell me that your bronze statue in Bologna is superb. You told me that you could not undertake such a work. Now it is highly praised. You are not aware of the scope of your talents."

Michelangelo realised that the Pope spoke in an ironic tone. He could hear the crowd sniggering.

"We have work for you here in Rome. It is important work and equal to your talents. It is our wish that you decorate the ceiling of the Sistine Chapel."

The crowd applauded.

The Pope studied his reaction carefully. Michelangelo grew pale. So the rumour was true.

"But I have no experience of frescoes. There are many others much more talented than your humble servant. This is a task that is beyond my powers."

"Enough of your protests. I am tired of your protests and your stubborn nature. You will decorate the ceiling. To begin with you will receive three thousand ducats. This should satisfy you. Now prepare for the task. This audience is at an end."

Michelangelo restrained his anger. "If it is your wish I shall undertake this impossible task." He bowed his head, rose from his kneeling position and, followed by Andrea, left the room.

Michelangelo and Andrea walked along the banks of the Tiber. The commission had imposed a dreadful weight upon the sculptor's mind.

"He asks me to do the impossible. Why not let Raphael undertake the task? He is a painter. Why am I the Pope's donkey. When will I sculpt again. When?"

Michelangelo was familiar with the Sistine Chapel. He knew the immense problems it posed. The ceiling was too high, the area he was required to cover too wide. He had to solve the problem of scaffolding. That alone was a difficult task. How long would he work in the ugly chapel? And all the while the blocks which had been hewn from the Carrara quarries lay like a white wall close to the Vatican. They went directly to the masons' square. The masons were working at their tasks. The air was filled with the music of iron on marble. The square had not been so busy in many years. Even the apprentices were allowed to carve their own pieces. Giovanni saw them enter the square. He left down his tools, wiped his hands on his apron and came towards them.

"You are welcome to Rome," he said.

"I note that you are busy," Michelangelo remarked.

"Never busier in my life. Thanks to Julius II we cannot keep up with the work. But sit down. Maria will bring you something to eat."

They sat on a long bench which was covered with marble dust. They looked at the workers. The place was as busy as a beehive.

Eventually Maria arrived with some food and a light wine. "So you have returned," she said.

"Yes. The Pope ordered me to return to Rome."

"To carve his tomb?"

"No. I have to paint the Sistine Chapel," he told her.

"You will do it. It is difficult but you will do it," she said and moved away.

"I would like to spend a week working here. It would give me a chance to think and I could clear my head," Michelangelo told Giovanni.

"This is humble work, not worthy of your talents."

"I respect marble. Every task is a worthy one. I have been given a gift. I can see the image in the stone. I can carve quickly and easily. But the Pope does not permit me to utilise this talent. Outside the Vatican lie the finest blocks of marble ever to come from Carrara. I am now commissioned to paint the Sistine Chapel. I cannot do it."

"Of course he can do it. I have seen some of his paintings. I have seen him learn the craft of bronze casting in a month," Andrea said.

"Are you for me or against me?" Michelangelo asked.

"I am always with you," Andrea replied proudly.

Michelangelo turned to Giovanni. "Will you come with me to the Sistine Chapel tomorrow? I want your advice on the scaffolding. You are experienced in such matters."

"Of course I will," Giovanni answered. "And how is Andrea progressing?"

"He has the gift and he uses it wisely. He has already sold his first panel of marble. When the ceiling is finished, I will give him one of the blocks to carve. It will stand on the tomb of the Pope."

"How long will the ceiling take?"

"It will be a rapid job. Nine months at most. My heart will not be in it. Once I solve a few problems I will begin."

But Andrea wondered about the nine months. He knew the workings of Michelangelo's mind. He would become obsessed with the ceiling. He would not rush the work once his mind was drawn into the task.

"What do you think, Maria?" Andrea asked her. She had returned from the kitchen and sat with them.

"I do not know. I have noted the care he takes

with everything. If he becomes obsessed with the ceiling, time will count for nothing."

"And the Pope. How will he get on with the Pope; will there be more trouble?"

"Who can say. If they keep away from each other, everything will be fine. But I expect that there will be some terrible scenes before all this is over."

"Yet the Pope has great respect for him."

"He has a most peculiar way of showing it."

"This commission could last for years."

"I know."

Maria decided that she would have to look after Michelangelo. She would have to keep his affairs and his lodgings in order.

They remained with the masons until evening. When the work of the day was finished and the marbles covered in wet cloth, they gathered about the large communal table. As always they spoke of marble and the great opportunities Rome now offered them. Michelangelo and Andrea enjoyed the company of the men. It was late when they said goodbye and made their way across the city to their lodgings.

Next day, true to his word, Giovanni arrived very early. He sat and ate with them. Then they set out for the Sistine Chapel.

They stood in the middle of the floor and looked at the building. On the walls was work by Botticelli, Rosselli and others. They studied the enormous space Michelangelo was required to fresco. The great arched ceiling was painted blue and covered with stars. It was high and wide like the sky. Michelangelo lay on the floor and looked at the ceiling. He had to fill this void with life and light. He felt like God on the first day of creation.

He began to think. Yes, he would paint panels of

the Apostles across the expanse. It was the simple answer to a difficult problem. He saw them ranged across the ceiling, each different, each with his own characteristics. Saint Peter with a grey beard and large fisherman's hands. Saint John with soft skin and mystical eyes and a gospel in his hand. Saint Matthew leaving a tax collector's office to follow Christ. The plan made sense.

The ideas poured into his mind. He would require several helpers to give him assistance, but he was capable of doing the work quickly.

While he was lying on the floor, a messenger from the Pope arrived. The Pope had found him accommodations which were spacious and equal to the task in hand.

They left the chapel and followed the messenger. The accommodations were indeed ample. However, when he inquired after the rent he was overwhelmed.

"It is too expensive. I will remain in my own quarters. I do not require palaces like Bramante and Raphael."

That evening Maria arrived. She set about ordering the place. Later she served them a meal. They ate the excellent food. All the time Michelangelo spoke of his plans for the chapel.

"And now I must find models. I must find men with character in their faces. I will sit in the masons' square and draw the workers. I noted that many of them suit my purpose."

"The masons in the square! You will find a gallery of saints and sinners there," Maria said laughing.

"Yes. That is what I will do," Michelangelo told them. "But before I study these models I must first construct the scaffolding. It will have to be moveable."

"We will help you," Giovanni agreed.

During the evening Giovanni suggested that Maria should become Michelangelo's housekeeper. Both he and his team of craftsmen would need food to sustain them during their arduous task. Michelangelo readily agreed with the idea.

A few days later they visited the chapel. In the centre stood the architect, Bramante, surrounded by noise and movement. Men had already built the scaffolding and were securing it with ropes. It was a rigid structure, cumbersome and unmoveable. It was secured to the ceiling by great poles which pierced the roof.

"What is going on here?" Michelangelo asked angrily. He disliked Bramante intensely. He was always dressed like a gentleman, had the ear of the Pope, and swaggered about Rome as if he were royalty. Michelangelo believed that he was plotting against him. He sensed that Bramante was behind the ridiculous commission he had just received.

"I am erecting the scaffolding for your commission," Bramante said.

"And who told you to do my work for me? Perhaps you wish to decorate the ceiling or are only the useless commissions thrown to poor artists?"

"The Pope instructed me to build the scaffolding."

"Did he give you permission to destroy the chapel, like you destroyed the old Saint Peter's?"

"What do you mean?"

"Are you blind? The roof has been destroyed. You have driven poles through the ceiling. What am I to do with these holes when I have finished?"

"Plaster them. Put gold leaf on them. It is not a significant commission. It will go unnoted."

"Nothing I do goes unnoted," Michelangelo said. "Now I order you to take down this monstrosity. If it is not taken down and the holes replastered, I will not begin the work."

"And how will you work on the ceiling? Fly up, no doubt, on one of these machines Da Vinci plans?"

"I have my own way of doing things."

"The scaffolding remains."

"Then I will leave."

"I will bring this to the notice of the Pope."

"Let us go to the Pope together. I will have this out with you once and for all. The fact that you are the architect for the new Saint Peter's does not mean that you can interfere with my work."

"Yes. Let us go. The Pope will decide."

As they walked along the corridor, Bramante turned to him in fury.

"Your scaffolding will collapse."

"No, it will not. I have given the matter much thought."

They were eventually given an audience with the Pope. Each gave his own point of view. Much to the surprise of the people present, the Pope favoured Michelangelo's ideas. Michelangelo returned to the Sistine Chapel alone. He called Bramante's carpenters.

"Take it down. Take everything down. Leave the poles on the floor and return to your master. No doubt he has work for you. He is favoured by the Pope. This idea of his was ridiculous. He is not a builder but a destroyer." He spoke in a loud voice in order that everyone would hear him. His words would be recounted to Bramante.

That evening he called Giovanni and drew a plan.

"The scaffolding can move and the ledges close to the top of the wall will bear some of the weight, like the arch of a Roman bridge," he explained.

"It is very clever," Giovanni said. "Why could I not

think of something like that?"

Michelangelo assembled a small group of carpenters. He gave them minute instructions and drew plans for them. It took a month to build the scaffolding.

When it was finished, he stood with Andrea and Maria and looked at the network of poles and ladders and platforms of timber.

"I am satisfied. We will begin the work in a week."

"And when will it be finished?" Maria asked.

"I do not know. But until it is finished it will be a burden about my neck."

They left the chapel and returned to the workshop. There was much work to be done.

The old man was excited. He had heard of the great task which would be undertaken by his neighbour. "How large is the ceiling?" he asked Maria.

"As large as a square," she told him.

"Is there paint enough in Rome to cover it?"

"We think there is."

"Will Michelangelo be able to cover this great ceiling with paint?"

"Yes."

"He's a hardy man, a hardy man."

Michelangelo spent a week preparing for the task. He set out his plans carefully.

Chapter 6

It was high summer. The heat was intense in Rome. Close to the city lay wide swamps in which fevers incubated. These were carried to the city. People became ill during the hot months. They complained of headaches and their lungs were choked. Frequently some fever or other broke out in the city. The weak and the old died.

During the hot months the rich left Rome. They possessed houses and palaces on the cool slopes of the mountains. In pleasure gardens, filled only with the sound of water falling and bird song, they whiled away their time in educated idleness. Here the air was sweet and life pleasant amongst trees and groves. Here they waited for the fevers to pass.

Michelangelo began to plan the cartoons for the Sistine Chapel during the hottest months of the summer. Every morning he left his lodgings followed by Andrea, who carried the rolls of paper which he used for sketching.

Usually Michelangelo remained silent as they made their way to the chapel. A huge task lay before him and his brow was furrowed in thought. He was undertaking a task which had never been attempted by another artist. He had to solve problems never faced by an artist before. Many thought that he could not complete the gigantic task and that he would fail in his effort. Sometimes he spoke to Andrea of the artist Raphael, who had just arrived in the city.

"He is related to Bramante, you know. He was brought here on his advice. How sweet and easy life is for him. Study his gorgeous paintings. They are delicious. Look at mine. They are tortured."

"The Pietà is sweet. Your David is noble."

"They were created during gracious times. I was in a happy mood. It is reflected in the work. Once I too was like Raphael. Now look at me. I am harassed."

"I will not listen to you, master. You never were like Raphael. Raphael borrowed from you. When he was in Florence he studied your work. Every dog in the streets of Florence knows that he was greatly impressed by your work."

"Look at him now. Commissions pour in his door. He works in delightful rooms in the Vatican. I work in a barn."

"You are the greater artist. People may not say it but they know it."

Michelangelo accepted the praise from Andrea. "I know what they say behind my back. They say that I will never finish the ceiling, that it is beyond my power. But I have the general plan in my mind and the ceiling will be finished."

"Will it take long, master?"

"Nine months. Perhaps ten, but we should be out of here within the year. Then I will return to Florence or maybe I will go to Venice, unless of course Julius permits me to begin his tomb."

"You mean his palace of the dead, master?" Andrea said.

"You have a wry sense of humour, Andrea. We need humour to keep us balanced."

They entered the chapel. It was as quiet as a mausoleum. The summer sun was shining through the windows and dust particles floated languidly on the bright shafts of light.

They climbed up the ladders and made their way onto the platform. The area about them was like a low extensive room. It was cool but soon it would become a furnace. The air was trapped between the platform and the roof.

Michelangelo studied the ceiling. Then, taking a sheet of paper, he made rapid outlines. Andrea was amazed at the certainty of his hand. The charcoal moved magically across the page, filling it with shapes. Time ceased for the artist. He did not require food or drink and he never relaxed.

Andrea realised that he was not required on the platform. He slipped down the series of ladders roped to the framework. He studied the paintings on the walls, particularly those of Botticelli. The work of the best masters in the world was all around him. Botticelli was the greatest of them all.

Andrea noted a door at the end of the chapel. He moved towards it and opened it. He was curious to find out what lay beyond. Passing through it he discovered a wide corridor. He did not know in what part of the Papal palace he stood. Moving forward on tiptoe, he was afraid that some guard might descend upon him with a drawn sword. At the end of the corridor he found an open door. He entered. An artist was working on a large painting. He recognised Raphael. He was not at all like Michelangelo in appearance. His skin was fine. There were no marks of tension or strain on his face. His brush stokes were easy and gentle. He was dressed in the fine clothes of a prince. He turned around and looked at Andrea. "Who are you?" he asked.

"Andrea is my name. I am apprenticed to Michelangelo."

"And where is your master?" asked Raphael.

"He is on the platform of the Sistine Chapel. He is setting out the plan for his frescoes."

"When I was young I studied his work in Florence. It was wonderful to behold. But he does not have the ability to paint the great ceiling. Fresco painting is not his trade. The Pope has set him too great a task."

Andrea grew angry but he controlled his feelings. "He will finish this work. Mark my words."

"But will it enhance his reputation?"

"His reputation is already enhanced. His Pietà and his David are the greatest sculptures in the world." He would have continued to defend his master's reputation but a Papal guard entered the room.

"Off with you. Raphael requires silence. You should not be here. You know that there are no artists comparable to him in Italy other than Leonardo da Vinci."

"What about Michelangelo? Have you not seen his Pietà in Saint Peter's?"

"He is only a stone mason."

"That is not correct."

"It is correct. And he lacks manners. He is ungainly at table. He is never invited to sup with the Pope."

"Manners have nothing to do with talent," Andrea replied.

The guard put his hand on his dagger. Andrea ran from the room and rushed down the corridor to the open door. He entered the Sistine Chapel. He mounted the platform. Beneath the ceiling it was now like an oven.

"You are tired, Master. You need rest and food," he said to Michelangelo.

"I cannot stop now. There is work to be done. Return to the lodgings and bring whatever food Maria has prepared. I will remain here. I must not lose a moment."

Andrea returned later with the food. While Michelangelo ate, his eyes never left the ceiling. He drank some milk and continued his work. He did not finish until late in the evening. The sun was setting when they left the Vatican Palace.

Michelangelo continued with his drawings for a week. During that time Andrea became familiar with the network of corridors which lay beyond the chapel. Sometimes he explored the warren of passages, at other times he sat before one of the paintings in the Sistine Chapel and copied from it.

"You have not wasted your time," Michelangelo said one day when he studied his paintings. "Your line is more certain now than it was and you have grasped the shape and balance of a work of art."

A week later Michelangelo was ready to begin the cartoons. These would be transferred to the ceiling.

He began to draw the cartoons in his workshop. A large sheet of paper was placed on an easel and with rapid strokes Michelangelo enlarged the drawings he had made in the chapel. They were teeming with life and action. He worked from morning till night on the images which he would transfer onto the ceiling.

Andrea and Maria were amazed at his energy. He could work for long hours and never grow tired. His small body was a bundle of artistic intensity.

"It is a pity that they will have to be destroyed," Andrea told Maria.

"Why?"

"In order to transfer them to plaster, you have to perforate the outlines and stencil them onto the wall with charcoal dust."

He took a piece of charcoal and drew a head. Then with a stylus he holed it. He held the transfer against the wall and dabbed the bag of charcoal dust against it. Then he removed the drawing. An outline appeared on the wall.

"That is how an outline is transferred to a wall," he told her proudly.

After some weeks Michelangelo believed that he had sufficient cartoons drawn to commence work on the ceiling. He sent to Florence for helpers who knew how to prepare plaster for the walls. Without them he could not transfer his images to the ceiling. They were received joyously when they arrived. Michelangelo had a warm affection for craftsmen from Florence. That night he held a supper for them. He invited Maria's father and the other masons from the square. The supper lasted until morning. They sang old Florentine songs and toasted each other's health.

"May we all soon return to our beloved city," Michelangelo told them.

"To Florence," they toasted.

A few days later they set out for the chapel. They had to plan their approach to the ceiling. These men knew the craft of fresco painting better than most. They had explained to Michelangelo how they would proceed in the workshop. One of them had prepared a demonstration.

First they coated a section of the wall with rough plaster called the *arriccio*. When it was dry, they covered it with a thin layer of finer plaster called the *intonaco*. The perforated cartoon was placed on the fine plaster and with a twig of charcoal the outline was marked out. Then the cartoon was drawn away and the outline made on the plaster which was still wet. The painting was then quickly executed.

"It must be painted while the plaster is wet. When it dries the colours are secured. They become lighter and they will last forever. The plaster forms a film over the colours and makes them glow," one of them explained.

Michelangelo was impressed by their experience.

They climbed the scaffolding. The chapel resounded to the sound of their shoes on the platforms and on the ladders. They surveyed the wide surface of the ceiling.

"It will have to be washed down," one of men said. "There is a coating of grease and smoke on the surface which has built up over the years. The ceiling must be prepared or the plaster will not hold."

A week later they were ready to begin the work. They filled a handcart with buckets, plaster, pigments and cartoons and set off for the chapel.

When they entered the chapel each man knew what was expected of him. The rough plaster had already been applied the day before and hatched so that the finer plaster would adhere to the surface.

They clambered up the series of platforms and reached the final level which stood just beneath the roof. They sat about on stools while the plasterer brought the mixture to its proper consistency.

Then with a deft hand he took a trowel and applied the plaster with long even strokes.

"This must be covered today," he told them.

They waited for it to harden a little. Then Andrea held the cartoon to the plaster and Michelangelo marked the outline. The cartoon was drawn away and the work started. Surrounded by brushes and pigments Michelangelo began the first day's work. The outline was filled in with quick brush strokes. On several occasions he had to be reassured by the craftsmen that the colours would take.

"Not only will they take but as the plaster whitens they will be sealed into the surface and radiate light."

The craftsmen were correct. When they returned next day, the plaster had dried. The pigments glowed beneath the surface.

They set up a pattern for their work and soon the first panel was finished. It spread across the ceiling in a magnificent fashion. It was a figure of strength and purpose. The whole plan was well balanced and the apostle had movement and character.

They studied their work and were satisfied with the result. They had spent a long time achieving this one figure and setting up their system of work.

"By any standards it is one of the best frescoes in Italy, I can assure you. I have been in this business for thirty years and I speak the truth," one of the workers said.

All agreed that it could not be improved upon. They asked Michelangelo for his honest opinion.

"What is done is done. But something annoys me about the whole thing. No, I don't like it. It will not fit into the general plan of the ceiling."

They looked at each other. "Have we wasted our time?"

"No. You have not wasted your time. I must think in terms of the whole ceiling. The whole ceiling must have a unity and a purpose. This is good in itself but it will not stand with others."

They were clearly confused at his talk.

"A figure is a figure is a figure. It is good or bad. This is good. Let Bramante or Raphael give their opinion," the plasterer suggested. Michelangelo grew angry. "Bramante and Raphael do not seek my opinion. I will not seek theirs!"

"Will we prepare another day's work?" the plasterer asked.

"No. Christmas is coming and it is time for a holiday. You must return to your families. I will give you a bonus which will see you through the holidays."

"Will you take a holiday?" someone asked.

"I do not know. There is much to consider."

They cleaned up the platform. They took the soiled cartoons, finger-stained and spotted with paint and plaster and tore them up. They swept the dust from the floor and carried it down the ladders in buckets. The chapel was closed for Christmas. They went back to the workshop. Following the instructions of Michelangelo, Maria had prepared a sumptuous meal for the craftsmen. It was a rich *stufato* or stew of meat and vegetables. This was washed down with red wine. Later, they sat about a fire and discussed all the business of the city. They had to admit that Julius II might not be a saintly man, but he was a man of excellent taste and was transforming the city. Some day Rome might approach Florence in beauty, one of them said.

Michelangelo disagreed. "That could never be. Florence is like a precious casket. It is neat and confined. Rome sprawls over seven hills."

The next day they said goodbye to Michelangelo, gave Maria a present, and set off in a jolly mood for Florence. Andrea accompanied them. Michelangelo had given him ten ducats. He instructed him to return in February when they would recommence the work.

Now the sculptor was alone. He returned to the workroom, threw some timber on the night embers and soon flames were climbing up the chimney. He looked into the centre of the flames, searching for an answer to a problem which was troubling him.

Maria, who was cleaning up the table, looked at him. He possessed a small figure and his face was sharp and intense. His broken nose gave him the expression of a brawler or a street fighter. She had grown very protective of Michelangelo. He seemed to care little for his appearance and wore the simplest of garments. He dressed like a peasant. Sometimes, when his mind was bent upon some idea, he forgot to eat. He looked unhappy and exhausted.

"What troubles you?" she asked.

"Ah Maria. You are still here. I thought you would be with your parents. You too must take a holiday. I can feed myself."

"No. You cannot. You look hungry and you look

unhappy," she said to him.

"Yes, I am unhappy. When I finished my Pietà and the bronze statue of Julius II, I knew that I had done my best. With the work in the Sistine Chapel I am not sure."

"I heard you say that it is a burden about your neck."

"It was, but I am becoming obsessed by it. A new plan is forming in my mind and it troubles me. It is magnificent beyond words. It would take much longer than I thought. I see the blocks I quarried in Carrara each day on my way to the chapel and I ask myself: when can I begin the task of sculpting?"

"You need a rest. You should leave Rome. Forget about art."

"You are young but you are wise. Your father and mother should be very proud of you. Yes, I must get away from this city. I must be alone."

Michelangelo spent Christmas day with Giovanni and his family. He was in a good mood. He had composed some songs which he sang for them and the conversation was of simple things. They did not speak of art or the Sistine Chapel, but of people they knew and the human troubles and joys which shake and shape life.

Soon after Christmas Michelangelo packed his bag and left Rome. He slung the bag across his shoulder and, taking a stout stick, set off towards the hills. It was cold and the sky was clear, but he did not feel the cold. His mind was occupied with the great ugly ceiling. How would he find the image which would link all his ideas?

He followed the path up through the hills. Beyond it lay the bare mountains, empty during the winter months. He decided that he would climb further up the steep flanks. Soon he was on the ridge of the mountain – the spine of Italy. The mountains ran to the south and to the north. The countryside was bare and austere. Beneath him in the valley he could see the comfortable habitations of man, with smoke rising lazily from chimneys.

Far away lay the enchanted sea, and where the arching sky met the sea was a weak indefinite line. He stood alone looking down on the scene. Then, for no reason at all, the opening lines of the Bible came into his mind: *God, at the beginning of time, created heaven and earth*.

The words' simple magnificence charged his mind with an image and then with other images.

He knew at that point the pictorial scheme for his work. It possessed the magnificence he sought. He would bring all things together in his ceiling: God and man, the great figures from the Bible and from the classics of Rome and Greece. He saw the hand of God outstretched, almost touching the figure of Adam, the first of the race.

Michelangelo spent a week in the mountains. He slept with the families of shepherds and peasants. He ate their simple food and drank their coarse wine.

When he crossed the Tiber in January, he had worked out the plan for the ceiling.

Winter had silenced Rome and no one was at war. He visited the Sistine Chapel and looked at the ceiling. He would have to remove the great fresco he had created and begin again.

He stood in the middle of the floor and looked up at the complex scaffolding which sustained the platform. He was trembling with excitement and fear.

Would he be able to bring the work to completion? How long would the endeavour take – two years? Perhaps more. He did not know. Of one thing he was certain. When the work was finished, nothing in the world would compare with it.

CHAPTER 7

The air was crisp. On the top of the barrel in the workyard was a layer of ice, like beeswax on a honeycomb. The sky was hazy and the light diffuse. Michelangelo's breath issued liked a plume from his mouth. The cold air sharpened his senses. He took some logs from the pile which stood against the wall and brought them indoors. He tore up some old drawings, bundled them up and placed them on the hearth. Then he arranged fine kindling about them, then heavier kindling, and on top of that branches. He lit the paper and soon the flames were playing above the timber. Later he set logs about them.

The ritual of the morning pleased him. Soon the room was warm. He ate some bread and sausage and drank light wine. His journey to the mountains had cleared his mind. Energy and urgency had returned to his body.

He took some sheets of rough paper and began to

sketch out his ideas in charcoal and made a general plan of the Sistine ceiling. To the side, in half moon-shaped frames and squares, he would place the prophets and the sibyls of Greece and, running the whole length of the chapel, majestic scenes from the Old Testament, beginning with the Separation of Light from Darkness and ending with the Drunkenness of Noah. In the centre he would position the creation of Adam on one panel and the creation of Eve on another. He was working on this grand plan when Maria entered the room. He did not hear her turn the key in the front door.

"I was passing," she said, "and I noted smoke rising from the chimney. I thought you had gone south?"

"I returned yesterday. I visited the chapel. Everything I have done must be removed."

"But I thought that the figure of the apostle was wonderful."

"It lacks beauty and nobility. It was hack work and that is unworthy of me. No. I have had a vision. I know what must be done. I have made the first general sketch."

Maria studied Michelangelo. He looked hungry. But then he always looked hungry. His face was gaunt and his eyes set deep in his sockets.

He invited her to study his plan. It looked impressive and clean.

"You work too hard. Your mind is on fire. Nobody can continue at your pace. You will burn out your energy. The people of Rome take it easy during the winter months. You, on the other hand, work as if there is no division between day and night."

"I have to. I must have the plans ready when the others return."

"And I must prepare a meal."

"I have left some money in the wooden box," he told her.

She set off for the market and soon returned with a basket of food. While Michelangelo continued his sketches, she diced the vegetables and the meat, placed them in a pot and set them to stew above the fire. Then she prepared the beds and freshened the rooms.

At midday Michelangelo stopped work and sat with her at the end of the table. He caught up on the family gossip and they chatted pleasantly for an hour.

"I did not realise I was so hungry," he said as he ate the rich stew. "I must visit Julius and get him to approve my plan. Nobody must see it but the Pope himself. Above all, Bramante must not see it. He got me into all this trouble. He would tell Raphael and Raphael would copy my ideas. I know that at present he is in search of ideas."

Michelangelo was obsessed with Bramante. He believed that all the bad luck which befell him was caused by the architect of Saint Peter's.

When the meal was finished he rolled up his plans.

"I must be off to see the Pope now," he said.

"But look at the way you are dressed; you should be ashamed of yourself. What will the Pope think?"

"Should I change?"

"Of course you should. You have not even cut your beard. You look like some wild man from the countryside."

"I forget about such matters."

"You will not make an impression on the Pope unless you are well presented."

He washed himself and changed his clothes, then Maria cut his beard.

"That looks much better," she said. "It is neat and pointed."

He wrapped himself in his winter cloak and set off with his plans rolled tightly under his arm.

When he reached the Vatican palace he was confronted by a cardinal. Michelangelo never knew the names of the cardinals.

"Whom do you seek?" the cardinal asked.

"The Pope."

"Have you arranged an audience with him?"

"No."

"The Pope is a busy man. The affairs of state weigh heavily upon him. You cannot walk in off the road and demand to meet him. We have procedures in the Vatican."

"I am also a busy man and the affairs of art weigh heavily upon me."

"Do you know who I am?" the cardinal asked.

"No. And I don't want to know."

"You are an arrogant man."

"And I do not suffer fools gladly. I have to see the Pope. You are obviously new here."

The cardinal grew angry. He would have called one of the guards to throw Michelangelo out of the palace but a secretary intervened. He wished to avoid a scene.

"Come with me, sir. The Pope will see you in a few minutes."

An hour later he was ushered into the presence of the Pope. He was busy dealing with his correspondence. "Well, what do you want?" the Pope asked brusquely.

"I would like to speak to you."

"Then speak."

"It concerns the chapel. I believe that what I have done is unworthy both of his Holiness and myself. I have come up with other plans."

"I am satisfied with your work."

"It lacks nobility. It has no dominant idea."

"I thought you hated the work. I have heard the rumour that you said you would be finished in nine months and that you found your task insufferable. You wish to be rid of Rome and your pontiff."

"I have said all these things. I have too free a tongue. But I cannot do work that is unworthy of me."

The Pope set down his quill and looked at the artist. There was a look of admiration in his eyes.

"Very well. Let me see your plan."

Michelangelo spread out the plan on the ornate desk. The Pope studied it carefully.

"This is magnificent. Truly, this is a superb vision of both God and man. God in his greatness, man in his greatness and his weakness. Nobody has ever had such a vision before. But can you accomplish this great task which you have set yourself?"

"I believe I can."

"Then in God's name, begin. I shall give you my blessing."

Michelangelo knelt down and the Pope blessed him. It was the first time in their acquaintance that the Pope had expressed appreciation of him. He left the palace in an cheerful mood and returned to the house.

"Was the Pope satisfied with your proposals?" Maria asked.

"More than pleased. He gave both me and the work his blessing."

"Then he was pleased," Maria said. Now that she was in charge of domestic affairs, she took a keen interest in all that was going on. She believed that the success of the undertaking depended as much upon her as upon Michelangelo.

They sat down at the wooden table and Maria served some food. She was an excellent cook and the room was filled with the aroma of good food.

During the week Andrea returned from Carrara. He wanted to catch up on all that had happened. Michelangelo told him of his vision on the mountain and of his visit to the Pope.

"How many assistants will you require for this work?" Andrea asked.

"None. We will do it together, you and I. The craftsmen are awkward. They cannot bring life to my cartoons. No. We will do it together. But the old work must be chipped away before we begin again. I will write to them and tell them of my plans. I know they will be displeased, but there is little I can do. Had I continued with the apostles, I would have done a second-rate piece of work."

That night by the firelight Michelangelo wrote a letter of explanation to the craftsmen. Next morning it was on its way to Florence with a bag of ducats.

A few days later he set off with Andrea for the Sistine Chapel. With fine chisels they chipped at the plaster until the large fresco of the apostle was obliterated.

"Now we can begin again," Michelangelo said.

They began to set out their plans. It was pleasant working in the empty chapel, with great shafts of light pouring in through the windows.

They arranged the bags of lime along the wall and the clay jars which carried the ground colours. They tested the pulley which would carry the wet lime to the platform. They were preparing the first coarse coat of plaster when a messenger arrived breathless from Maria.

"The workers have come from Florence. They wish to see you. They are in a dark mood."

"Tell Maria that I have no wish to see them. I will

bolt the door and will not leave this place until they have left." With that he locked the door and they set about applying the first rough coat of plaster. Michelangelo smoothed it onto the vault. Then he held a cartoon close to it. "It matches. Tomorrow I will apply the fine wet plaster. Then I will have to work furiously to finish the first day's work."

They were busily engaged in the work when they heard a banging on the door.

"Michelangelo! Michelangelo! We know that you are within. We have come to help you. You cannot accomplish this task alone."

The heavy thumping on the door echoed in the great chamber. Michelangelo did not answer them.

"I have paid them well. Why do they pester me?" he asked.

Then there was silence. They began the work again. That evening the knocking commenced once more. It was louder this time and the men called out in drunken voices.

"We will have to remain here for the night," Michelangelo told Andrea. Night came and they wrapped themselves in old blankets which they had brought with them.

Late in the night there was a lighter knocking on the door.

"It is I, Maria. They have left. You can come out now."

It was late when they made their way across the city. Most Romans were in bed except for a few revellers who were returning from a wedding in the countryside.

The next morning they returned to the chapel.

"Today we begin with the Deluge," Michelangelo told Andrea as they set about mixing the fine plaster.

Then Michelangelo mounted the platform and hauled up the bucket of fine plaster.

Andrea watched the first bucket move ceilingwards. It would be the first of many thousands which would be lifted onto the platform. Michelangelo applied the plaster finely like a craftsman. Andrea was amazed at how quickly he could master a craft. They permitted the lime to dry a little, then they pinned on the cartoon and Andrea dusted the perforations with charcoal dust. When this was removed, Michelangelo began his work on the Sistine Chapel. He quickly filled in the outline, and then, with masterful strokes, began to paint in the figures. The small plan which he had sketched in the workshop was now being transferred to the ceiling. They worked all day in the confined space.

"If this fails then I must begin again," he said when he was finished.

It was only a small section of the great panel. Already it had begun to dry into the plaster.

"Tomorrow we will know if it has taken or not. We will not apply further rough plaster until I am certain of the technique."

It was evening when Maria arrived with warm food in a crockery jar. She mounted the platform and gazed at the work.

Andrea explained to her what they were about.

"Find someone who can mix and apply the plaster. It will take the hard labour from the task and you can remain at home preparing the cartoons," she said.

"But I wish to do the whole thing myself," Michelangelo told her.

"There is bound to be a plasterer you can trust," she said.

"I will think about it."

That night they sat about the fire and wondered if the colours were drying with the plaster.

"Once Leonardo painted a magnificent wall but he used a new technique which had not been tested before. The colours ran," he told them.

"You are using tried techniques," Andrea told him. "You will not fail."

"Once I am certain of the practice, I can set about the work."

Next morning the three of them entered the chapel. They were apprehensive as they mounted the platform. But when they studied the work they were certain that they had succeeded. The colours had set into the plaster and were glowing with a rich light.

"It is lit from within," Maria remarked.

"The ceiling will fill the eye with wonder," Andrea added.

"When it is finished," Michelangelo said. "Now I have to get a good plasterer. I am sure there is one in the city."

"My father will know," Maria said.

Two days later the plasterer arrived at the workshop. He was a small lumpy man with a bulbous nose. He possessed an engaging expression and a smile played on his lips.

"I am the best plasterer in Rome if all were known," he said. "I work hard and I have a large appetite. Feed me well and you will get good work from me. I know the art of fresco plastering. I work evenly. There is never a mark or a water bubble on my surfaces."

"Then I will engage you," Michelangelo said.

"Good. I smell food. Now I will eat."

Maria brought him a large dish of stew. When he was finished he asked for more.

"I will return in a week and study your cartoons. I

will judge how much you can do each day. I will prepare the rough plaster and early in the morning I will apply the fine plaster. I will leave the chapel as the Dominican bell rings. One hour later the plaster will be ready to receive paint. You must trust my judgement in these matters."

Michelangelo gave him five ducats as he left.

"Thank you, kind sir. Such money is welcome." He left and ambled down the street.

"He is the man I was looking for," Michelangelo said.

"He has eaten all our food," Maria said. "I have never known a small man with such an appetite."

"He is worth his food," Michelangelo told her. "Now we must begin the cartoon of the Deluge. We will have to enlarge it to fit the panel."

The rhythm of work was beginning to take shape. They worked out the forms for the Deluge. Michelangelo recalled the Arno in spate when trees were uprooted from the ground, bales of straw and animals carried downstream and the terror which had possessed people's faces. These images and many other images of the past began to crowd in upon him. A great raft-like ark floated towards the horizon, secure against the elements. In a corner men, women and children sought the higher ground. On the left others sought the security of a rocky ledge. All the faces were filled with terror, fear and despair.

When the cartoon was finished, they pinned it to the wall. They had to curl in the edges in order to accommodate it. They stood at the end of the room and gazed at the work. It was a massive beginning to the great task.

"And now we must cut it into sections," Michelangelo said.

They called the plasterer. After a good meal he cast his professional eye on the cartoon.

"I have the rough plaster spread across the space the cartoon will occupy. Now we must judge to the hour how much you can accomplish each day." With these words the plasterer left, promising to return later in the day.

It took them some time to decide. Michelangelo and Andrea visited the chapel and mounted the platform. Lying on their backs, they surveyed the grey plaster.

"Yes. I know how much we will be able to finish each day." Michelangelo took a stick of charcoal and marked out a section on the ceiling. "Prepare the plaster and apply it. We will return in an hour's time," he ordered.

They returned to the chapel an hour later. They were eager to set about their task. The plaster was drying and they placed the cartoon against it. Immediately the outline was marked off, the cartoon taken down and set aside and then the work began. Andrea stood beside Michelangelo while he worked rapidly on a face. He brought out the anguish and fear of the character, then he began to colour in the cartoon, calling to Andrea to mix the colours as they were required.

They worked all day without a break. When the section was finished, Michelangelo's beard and shirt were spotted with paint. His face was drawn and the muscles of his arms ached. He lay on his back and studied what he had done.

"I am satisfied. The breath of the Spirit is blowing through it."

When the plasterer returned that evening, he studied the work with a professional eye. "It is perfect," he said. "It will dry during the night and tomorrow morning I will apply the next section of plaster."

They were weary as they descended the platform. It was almost dark and they carried a lantern. They locked the chapel and returned to the house. Maria had prepared their evening meal. They were exhausted after the day's work and ate in silence.

"Well," she asked finally. "How did the work go today?"

"Very well," Michelangelo replied. "I am beginning to grasp the technique of the fresco worker."

"There will be no ceiling in the world like it," the plasterer said when he had consumed his large meal.

"We have much to do and to accomplish," Michelangelo told them. "I sometimes wish I had not undertaken such a task."

"Count yourself lucky. At least you are gainfully employed," the plasterer said. "I know several artists in Rome who cannot find employment." He clearly did not understand the importance of Michelangelo. He noted that some stew remained in the pot. "I might as well eat it if it is there. Waste not want not," he said. While he ate he concentrated all his energies on his food.

They watched in amazement as he ate the second large helping of food.

"I tell you he will eat us out of house and home," Maria said when he had departed.

The next morning, as the bells of the Dominican church sounded over the city, they entered the chapel with a section of the cartoon. The plasterer had finished his work and was cleaning his trowel.

So began the second day. The work on the fresco moved forward. They encountered no difficulties. The great painting began to take on life. The fresco extended across the arch of the chapel. The colours were bright and filled with light.

Then it happened. One morning they mounted the stairs and gazed at the work. It was marked with black and green stains. Fungus had began to grow like some evil disease on the surface of the plaster.

Michelangelo turned to the plasterer.

"My work has been destroyed. I thought you knew your job! Can you account for what has happened?"

"I have been up and down Italy plastering walls but this has never happened before."

"Well it has happened now," Michelangelo replied curtly.

"It shouldn't have happened," the plasterer protested.

"But it has. This is the end of my work. My reputation is in shreds. Won't Bramante and Raphael have a good laugh at me now? I can hear their sarcastic laughter in my ears. I must tell the Pope what has happened. I will give up this work and leave the city."

Andrea thought that his master might cry. Michelangelo rushed down the stairs. Andrea followed him. He pulled open the door which led into the Vatican palace and moved rapidly along the corridors. He reached the private rooms. He banged upon the door.

A secretary told him that he could not see the Pope. "I must see him," he said and brushed him aside.

"Let him in," the Pope called. "He sounds like a spirit in torment." Michelangelo stood before the Pope.

"Well what brings you here so early in the morning?"

"The fresco is destroyed. Fungus is growing on the surface. It will feed on the colours. I should not have undertaken the task," he blurted out.

"Calm down. Have a glass of wine. All may not be lost. I will call Sangallo. He is well versed in these matters. He will give us his opinion."

Sangallo was sent for. He came immediately to the Pope's quarters.

"Michelangelo has a problem with his fresco," Julius said. "Fungus is growing on the surface. Examine it and give me your opinion."

"Yes, your Holiness," said Sangallo, bowing.

Michelangelo left the apartments and paced the corridor for half an hour. He kept repeating to himself, "It is a disaster. It is a disaster. Nothing can save the work."

Sangallo returned. There was little on his face which would indicate that he had solved the problem. He entered the apartments with Michelangelo.

"Well?" the Pope asked. "What is your opinion?"

"It is not as bad as you thought. The plaster was too wet. It is perfect for a normal wall but on the ceiling of the Sistine Chapel it needs to be much drier. When the plaster dries properly, the fungus will disappear."

"Good. Then the work can continue."

"Yes."

The Pope turned to Michelangelo. "Return to your work. This may be your crowning achievement."

They returned to the chapel. The plasterer was sitting on a rough stool, his head bent in shame.

"Cheer up," Michelangelo said. "The world has not come to an end. Your plaster is too wet for these conditions."

The fat plasterer with the lumpy face looked up and smiled. "And I thought my reputation was destroyed. There are those in Rome who would also laugh at me. Plastering is a jealous profession."

With the problem settled, a new energy seemed to

possess Michelangelo. He worked from morning until night on the fresco of the Deluge. His face grew gaunt and the lines on his forehead deeper. He forgot to eat and only at evening time did he have his meal.

"He will die of hunger," Andrea told Maria one evening.

"We will all soon die of hunger. He thinks only of the ceiling. I have no money left. He has no regard for money. Look at Raphael. He is wealthy beyond measure. Everybody respects him because he charges large fees for his commissions. He is a companion to the Pope and accompanies him on tours about the city and sits at his table. Michelangelo on the other hand, is as poor as a beggar and looks like one. Somebody will have to do something about it."

"Leave it to me," Andrea said.

The next day when Michelangelo had begun his work high on the platform, Andrea slipped out of the chapel. He moved along the familiar corridors. He arrived before the Pope's office. He took up courage and knocked at the door. The Pope's secretary looked out.

"Who are you?" he asked. "How did you escape the guards at the end of the corridor?"

"I know my way about the palace and I was desperate to see the Pope."

The secretary looked at him more carefully. "You are the apprentice who works with Michelangelo," he remarked.

"That is correct," said Andrea.

The Pope had heard the conversation. "Permit him to enter," he directed. The Pope was in a good mood and less fearful in appearance than normal. He placed his fingers on his stomach and locked them together. "Well, what can I do for you, young man? Ambassadors have to wait weeks to have an audience with the Pope. You stroll in as if your were at home."

Andrea knelt down and bowed his head. "I come on a matter of great urgency, your Holiness. I come on behalf of Michelangelo. We have no money left and we have almost run out of food. My master is not aware of these things. He does not eat enough and he thinks only of the Sistine Chapel. He says the winds of the Spirit are blowing through his mind but, your Holiness, the winds of hunger are blowing through the rest of us."

The Pope began to chuckle. He asked Andrea many questions concerning himself. It was a pleasant encounter.

"You are a good ambassador for your master. You explained exactly why you came and you did not beat about the bush. I wish my cardinals could be so direct. They certainly will not die of hunger. I will direct my secretary to give you ten ducats. If you require more let him know. Now, tell me how the work in the chapel proceeds."

"Very quickly. I have never known my master to be more certain of what he is about. Since the problem of fungus was solved, it is impossible to prevent him from working. I fear for his health. He has undertaken a magnificent commission. But it is arduous work. He thinks only of this vision he must commit to the ceiling."

"I know. He is a simple, religious man. That is why the winds of God blow through his mind. Some day he will thank me for this commission. He complains that he is taken from his true vocation, but God writes straight on crooked lines. Go return to your work. Do not let him know that this conversation has taken place."

The secretary gave Andrea the ten ducats. He returned quickly to the chapel.

"Where were you?" Michelangelo called from the ceiling.

"Here and there. I had a walk through the palace."

"There is work to be done, Andrea. I need some strong ochres. Come quickly!"

Andrea clambered up the steps to the platform, afraid that this master might hear the jingle of gold in his pocket. That night they ate well. The great work proceeded apace.

CHAPTER 8

Rome spoke only of Raphael, the young and talented artist. He was honoured by both the Pope and the cardinals. A young man of fine skin and polished manners, he was welcomed at the palaces of the wealthy. He was overwhelmed with commissions and he could demand high fees for his work.

The Romans rarely spoke of Michelangelo. Few paid attention to him. He was too intense and fiery, too private about his work, beggarly in appearance and possessing little wealth. He did not cut a dash and was therefore looked down upon. Rome loved pomp and ceremony. Michelangelo did not belong to its ways.

He continued the long and demanding work on the Sistine Chapel. He seemed like a man possessed, living in the world of the Bible rather than in Renaissance Rome. He frequented the roughest taverns in search of portraits for his work. Many believed that he would die before he completed his work, or at least would grow old in the pursuit of perfection.

The Deluge had been completed – a work of great movement and energy. It was supported by two crescent-shaped paintings of Zorobabel and Josiah. They were fine and firm. Now Michelangelo began the second panel. It would deal with the drunkenness of Noah. He had now fallen into a pattern of work and worked quickly on the fresco. Each morning the plasterer had his work finished when they entered the chapel. Andrea then prepared the colours in the clay dishes. After he had helped Michelangelo apply the cartoon, it was his job to mark in the outlines, while the artist wet the paints and applied egg white to bind them. Once they had marked out the outline and taken away the cartoon, the work began. They often spoke of the subject in hand.

"It shows Noah in a very poor light," Andrea said as he looked at the old bearded man lying beside a large wine barrel.

"My ceilings show man as he is and man as he might be. Wait until we have completed the creation of Adam. It will be a great generous figure. I see it in my mind's eye."

The monotonous work continued. They did not think of the blank space which lay ahead of them.

Eventually the fresco of Noah was finished. Sloping down from the central panel he would place the figures of Joel and Delphica; one a prophet, the other a Greek figure. Andrea had been with him when he had discovered the faces at a vegetable market.

"All Greek and Jewish learning must be brought together on my ceiling. They have served each other well. They have served me well. They have lit up our world with great lamps."

Julius II had remained far from the chapel during the work. Now he expressed a desire to see how far Michelangelo had progressed.

"We hear a lot of talk and many more rumours," he said to the artist. "We must see the work. We must find out if our money has been well spent."

"Perhaps you will not be able to climb the ladders," Michelangelo told him, hoping that his suggestion might prevent the Pope from visiting him on the ceiling.

"You try and fob me off, Michelangelo. If I cannot climb the ladders, then you will have to haul me on high in a basket. I am determined to see this work which has been hidden from me and everyone else in Rome."

"Very well. Take it easy. Some of the steps on the ladders are weak. They will not take a heavy weight."

"I will not be put off. I will reach the ceiling or die in the attempt." Julius made the strenuous ascent. He worked his way from level to level, calling Andrea to bring him a stool so that he could sit down and rest. He had to rest frequently in order to gain his breath. Finally he arrived on the platform. There were beads of perspiration on his forehead and a grey pallor on his skin.

He raised his eyes to the ceiling. They filled with delight when he saw the frescoes. He sat on the stool and examined each section of the work with an appreciative eye. Andrea realised that he was more than a soldier Pope. His eyes had been well trained and he recognised beauty and genius when he saw it. He followed every line and lingered over each feature.

"Now I understand why you abandoned your first

plan. This great idea of yours has meaning. Philosophers and prophets and the greatest moments from the Bible are drawn easily together. I am pleased with your work."

"Thank you, your Holiness. I try and serve my Pope as well as I can."

"This is a new departure for you. When will it be finished?" he asked.

"I do not know. I have only begun. Here there is light and colour, but look at the great empty space I have yet to cover." The painter directed his attention to the wide space behind them.

"In the beginning, when God created the universe, the earth was formless and desolate. The raging ocean that covered everything was engulfed in total darkness and the Power of God was moving over the darkness," the Pope chanted. Then he was silent for a moment. He considered the work that remained to be done. "You play the part of God on this platform," he said.

"And down there on the floor I am like one of God's beggars," the artist replied.

"I understand. I can take a hint. You need money. I will have five hundred ducats sent to you."

"I am most grateful to you," the artist replied.

"Keep up the good work. I would prefer to be up here in your company than in the Vatican Palace. My enemies surround me. They plan to capture Rome and take me prisoner. The Pope is no longer a sacred figure. I must prepare for war. When will I have peace to enjoy my gardens or walk through the vineyards? I carry a heavy burden. My enemies would destroy the church for their own ends."

"It is founded upon a rock and will not falter," the artist told him.

"Well, at present it is beaten by high storms."

"They will pass. Soon the skies will clear."

"I wonder . . . "

There was a note of weariness in the Pope's voice. Michelangelo studied his features. Julius was growing old. The continual wars were wearing him down. His figure was stooped.

He rose from the stool.

"I must return to earth," he said. Julius rose slowly and made his way to the ladder. Michelangelo watched the pontiff climb down the stairs. Soon he became a small figure. He watched him shuffle out of the building. Michelangelo turned to Andrea.

"He is pleased with my work. That gives me great satisfaction. And we have money at last. You can send twenty ducats to your parents; that will please them. Maria can be paid and we can afford to treat ourselves to a feast; we will invite the old man and offer him wine blessed by the Pope. He has lost some of his courage I note."

"Why not bring him to the chapel some day? He would like that. It would give him much to talk about."

"An excellent idea! Yes, we must cheer him up."

The visit from the Pope had restored Michelangelo's energy and his confidence. Ideas flooded into his mind.

Once the debts were paid, Maria was able to provide them with good food. The old man came to visit them. He drank some wine which they said had been blessed by the Pope.

"You must visit us in the chapel some day. We need your advice," Michelangelo said.

"If I can be of any service, I will gladly give my opinion. I have seen much, in my time, on land and on sea."

Michelangelo began to work on the next panel: the sacrifice of Noah. It was a complicated and clever piece of work and much more confident than the first two panels. Then one day Michelangelo turned to Andrea and said, "I had a feeling this morning when I came into the chapel that we had had a night visitor."

"But nothing is disturbed, master."

"I know somebody was here. Is there no peace from prying eyes?"

"Tonight I will keep watch in the chapel. I will sleep in a corner. If there is a night visitor, I will discover who it is," said Andrea.

"A very good idea. If there is more than one, listen to their conversation. Find out what they are about."

"Yes, master."

They built a small partition close to the wall and arranged a rough mattress. "You will not be afraid?" Michelangelo asked as he prepared to leave the chapel.

"No, master."

Michelangelo closed the chapel door. Andrea felt lonely. The place grew dark. He tried to sleep but could not. He heard mice darting about the scaffolding. They scratched and gnawed at things. Then his imagination began to play tricks on him. He thought perhaps that some ghost from the past might visit the chapel. He had heard of spirits haunting holy places. Late in the night, half asleep and half awake, he heard a door creaking. He rose from his bed and peered over the partition. He could see two figures. They carried a lantern with a steady flame. They climbed the ladders. The lantern threw ghostly shadows on the wall. They spent some time on the platform. He could hear the echo of their voices but he could not make out their words. Then they descended the ladders. He recognised both figures. Bramante and Raphael had come to visit the chapel.

Andrea was exhausted when they left. He threw himself out on the mattress, pulled a blanket over his head and fell asleep.

Michelangelo shook him awake. "Well, had we visitors?" he asked.

"Yes. Bramante and Raphael."

"Thieves! I could have guessed that it was the two of them," Michelangelo cried. "They have come to steal my ideas. Now Raphael will imitate me and will be paid well for the imitations. They stole from me in the past and they will steal again. The Pope must hear about this. I will not tolerate such an intrusion. I am a private person. I do not stick my nose into their business."

Michelangelo's eyes were flaming with anger. He rushed from the chapel and down the corridor.

Andrea followed him. "Be careful, master. Do not lose your temper. You may live to regret it."

"I will not be careful. The time has come to face my enemies. They spread nasty rumours about me all over Rome."

When the guards saw him approach, they pointed their spears at his heart.

"Go ahead, kill me if you wish, but you will have to account for my death to the Pope."

They hesitated. He brushed their lances aside and walked past them. He sought an audience with Julius and waited anxiously outside the door until he was called.

"Well, what is your problem?" the Pope asked.

"I am spied upon. Last night Andrea slept in the chapel. He saw Bramante and Raphael mount the platform. They have no business in the chapel. I do not poke my nose into their affairs. They have come to steal my ideas, your Holiness."

Julius turned to Andrea. "Are you sure of this?"

"I am certain, holy father. I could not fail but recognise them."

"Very well, I believe you." Julius called his secretary. "Bring Bramante here immediately. I will have words with him." Bramante arrived quickly. His face was flushed. He knelt before the Pope.

"Did you visit the Sistine Chapel last night?"

Bramante hesitated for a moment.

"I have asked you a question," the Pope said angrily. "I expect an answer and I expect the truth."

"Yes, your Holiness."

"Who was with you?"

"Raphael."

"What business brought you to the chapel?"

"I wished to study the structure of the building."

"Liar," called Michelangelo in anger. "You came to steal my ideas. You are a thief!"

The guards restrained Michelangelo until his anger waned.

"Give your key to Michelangelo. I forbid you or anybody else to visit the chapel. Do you understand?"

"Yes, your Holiness."

"Keep far from me, Bramante," said Michelangelo, "or I will throttle you. I am not interfering with your destruction of Saint Peter's; no wonder the population of Rome call you Ruinante."

It was now Bramante's turn to lose his temper. He looked at Michelangelo with hate in his eyes. "You are a peasant without manners. You lack charm and grace. Who would have you at their table?" he said.

"Saint Peter lacked grace, yet Christ made him his successor."

It was now the turn of the Pope to lose his temper. "Stop or I will throw both of you in the dungeons of Castel Sant' Angelo. That will cool your tempers."

The Pope's anger frightened them. He spoke to them sternly. "It is your business to make Rome a beautiful city. I have enough trouble on my shoulders without having to come between two artists when they quarrel and abuse each other. You are a disgrace to your professions. Remove yourselves from my presence. Return to your respective works." He ordered his soldiers to show them back to their quarters.

"Peasant!" Bramante called after the departing figure of Michelangelo.

"Ruinante!" Michelangelo replied.

Maria was waiting for them when they returned to the chapel. Andrea explained what had happened. Maria burst out laughing. Andrea began to laugh. Even Michelangelo had to smile.

"That will put manners on both of you," she said as they sat down for a meal.

They continued working on the Sacrifice of Noah. Michelangelo was preoccupied with his work. His mind was fired with ideas and inspiration. He had become engrossed in the ceiling.

"The Spirit is blowing through my mind," he often said. "He urges me forward."

The plasterer was told to extend the area of work. In order to hasten the work, Michelangelo carried a mattress onto the platform. When Andrea descended the ladders each evening, Michelangelo continued to work. His beard grew long and grey. Dark circles formed under his eyes and his face became rutted with lines. He grew old quickly. He no longer washed and there was a stench from his body.

Andrea worried about his health. He forgot to eat. Plates of half-eaten food lay about the platform.

"He is growing old, Maria," Andrea told her one evening. "And smelly. Does he expect me to wash his clothes? The beggars of Rome smell more sweetly. What shall we do?"

"He is a stubborn man," Maria said, "possessed with a burning idea. He will not even listen to the Pope."

One day Andrea brought Michelangelo a letter from his father in Florence. Michelangelo sat down and opened it. He could not read it. The letters seemed to dissolve on the page.

"I am growing blind," he cried. "I can barely see. I have worked too close to the ceiling. And my head is reeling." He held his head as if it were about to burst.

"It is time to rest, master," Andrea told him.

He helped Michelangelo down the ladders and he locked the chapel door. He led the artist home.

When Maria saw Michelangelo she was amazed at the change which had taken place. His beard was grey and filthy with paint. His clothes were ripped and torn. He was exhausted. He undressed and washed. Then a great tiredness descended upon him. He fell into bed and slept for three days.

"He carries too heavy a burden," Giovanni told them. "Let him sleep. His strength will return. He is made of iron. He may look small but he has the energy of a lion."

Three days later Michelangelo awoke. His sight had returned and his mind was clear.

He put on new clothes which Maria had purchased and sat down to a large meal.

"Now I have to paint the Tempation and the Expulsion," he said when he was finished.

"But you must take it easy," Maria told him. "Walk in the mountains. It will refresh your spirit."

"I cannot rest. Raphael and Bramante may rest but I cannot," he said. "I must continue with the work."

With that he left the table and entered the large workroom. He unrolled the half-finished cartoon of the Temptation and Expulsion and studied it. Then, taking a piece of charcoal, he began to work on it. His strokes were quick and certain.

He called Andrea and told him to find a certain passage in the Bible.

"Now read it to me," he said.

Andrea began to read slowly: *"Now the snake was the most cunning animal that the Lord God had made. The snake asked the woman, 'Did God really tell you not to eat fruit from any tree in the garden?'"*

"Read it again," Michelangelo ordered.

While Andrea read the passage, Michelangelo continued his work. Later Andrea studied the cartoon. Adam and Eve were more noble than anything yet created for the ceiling. They were both in possession of Eden. Their bodies were beautiful, perfect in every way. Coiled about the tree, with the tail of a serpent and the torso of a man, was the Devil tempting Eve. He was handing her the fruit of both good and evil. Beyond the tree Michelangelo drew the scene of banishment. A fiery angel could be seen driving them out into a barren world. They moved forward, timid and afraid. Every part of the picture was well-balanced and unified.

"Tomorrow we start our work again," Michelangelo told Andrea and Maria.

In the morning they set out for the chapel. Andrea

pushed a small handcart with the cartoon and some bowls of paint. Michelangelo, dressed in a rough cloak, looked like a peasant. His face was intense and his mind was upon his work. When they were passing across one of the squares, Raphael, resplendent in fine clothes and surrounded by a retinue of admirers, approached.

They began to laugh at the appearance of both Michelangelo and Andrea.

"They are selling vegetables it appears," Raphael said in a loud voice. With bowed heads the two passed them by without saying a word.

When they had passed out of the square, Michelangelo turned to Andrea. "He is a lucky man I can assure you. Had I not important work to do, I would have broken his jaw. I detest arrogance."

"You did the correct thing, master," Andrea said.

"No I did not. If I had any sense I would have taken him by the throat and throttled him. I do not have to take insults from an upstart like him. Before he knew what a piece of charcoal was, I had already accomplished acclaimed works."

Michelangelo mounted the platform and began his work.

"I will show Raphael and Bramante that I did not come to Rome to sell vegetables. Had I lost my temper, I would have split his jaw with my fist. He is soft. Look at my hands. They are sculptor's hands, hard as iron."

The humiliation served on him by Raphael charged him with new determination. He sent Andrea to find the plasterer to prepare a larger surface. He would work through the night if necessary in order to catch up on lost time.

There was only a short break for a meal. While

others took their siestas, Michelangelo worked like a man possessed by some demon. He was driven forward by an enormous energy.

"It has to be the spirit of God moving through him," Andrea often told Maria. "Creation pours from his hands. He rarely has to change a line."

"Will he ever be finished, Andrea?" Maria asked.

"Yes. Some day he will put down his brushes and he will say, 'It is done. Let us return to the marble blocks.'"

"Will you be as great as Michelangelo?"

"Nobody will ever be as great as Michelangelo, but I will have learned my craft from him."

Before he left the platform, Andrea prepared the lanterns for his master. They would burn during the night.

Michelangelo returned to his old habits. His beard grew long and untidy and was matted with paint. A huge goitre had formed in his neck and his body became twisted from working in such a confined space.

Then one night, as Maria and Andrea were sitting by the fire, Michelangelo entered the room like a drunkard reeling from too much wine.

"It is finished! The Temptation and the Expulsion is finished. The first parents now roam through the desolate world."

"Do you require food?" Maria asked.

"Yes bring me food and drink."

"Not until you have washed and put on new clothes. You stink to the high heavens."

Michelangelo obeyed her meekly and returned to the table washed and refreshed. He wore a new blue tunic which Maria had purchased in the markets. He did not speak to them. Instead he ate his food mechanically and drank his wine in awkward gulps and gazed at the wall.

"And now I must prepare for the next fresco. It will deal with the creation of Eve. I have the total picture in my mind. A kind and wise God draws her from Adam's side. She will be a beautiful woman because she is the mother of all mankind. Adam will sleep by a tree while God draws her from his side."

"Can you not take a rest from your labour?" Maria asked.

"It is no longer a labour. It has become a passion. I now sculpt people on the ceiling and not out of marble. Study them. They are sculptures."

It was something which Andrea had observed many months ago. Michelangelo slept fitfully during the night. Andrea heard him call out in his sleep. When he woke in the morning his master was already at work sketching out plans for the new panel.

"Find the plasterer. Bring him to me. Tell him I need him."

The plasterer arrived. He was tired and angry.

"You told me that I could have a week off," he complained.

"I need you now."

"I need a rest. I am human. I have to visit my family in the north. My wife sends complaining messages to me. She is a woman with a fiery temper. I must go and visit her." With that he left the room.

"What will I do?" he asked Andrea and Maria.

"I can mix the plaster. I have watched him often enough. If I can mix dough and roll it out for pies, I can mix and spread plaster," Maria said with confidence.

"It is worth a try," Michelangelo said. "We must keep going."

They set off for the chapel with the cartoon. Maria mounted the platform, trowelled out some dry plaster, mixed it as she had seen the plasterer do and applied it to the wall evenly. They watched it dry.

"Excellent. You must come and work with us," Michelangelo said.

Dressed as a boy, she set off each morning and plastered the ceiling in preparation for the cartoon. Then she returned home and prepared the food.

When the Creation of Eve was finished she stood with the others and admired the work.

"It is indeed beautiful. Now I know why you go without food and sleep in order to finish such a noble thing," she told Michelangelo.

He smiled at her.

"So you begin to understand at last."

"Yes."

He was pleased with the work. The panels fitted into a sequence. The artist had worked backwards from the Drunkenness of Noah. The final fresco would be the Separation of Light and Darkness, the first one in the sequence.

"We have more than half our task completed," he told them. "I have spent two years in this confined place, hell you might call it, painting the roof of heaven. I have endured the heat and the cold. I have been hungry and thirsty, dirty and ill, but we have kept going. Now I can see the end. The day will come when we will lay down our brushes, dismantle the platform and the Pope and Raphael and Bramante and the whole world will see what has been achieved in such a prison – for this place is a prison."

It was the longest speech Michelangelo had ever made. It was filled with passion and they felt tears start to their eyes.

The next day Michelangelo began to concern himself with the central panel: the creation of Man. He would not begin it immediately. Instead he would work on the minor frescoes which lay to the side of the main panels.

He was working on the figure of Ezekiel when he heard somebody mount the ladders.

"Who is there?" he called.

"Your Pope," came the reply.

"It is dangerous up here," he called down.

"Not as dangerous as the field of battle," the Pope replied.

He arrived on the platform. Michelangelo knew that he was in one of his crusty moods.

"When will this ceiling be finished? Or will it ever be finished?" he asked.

"It will be finished when it is finished," Michelangelo replied. He too was in a crusty mood.

The Pope raised his stick and brought it down on Michelangelo's back. "You are an arrogant fellow to speak to your Pope in such a manner," he said.

Michelangelo clenched his fist. He was going to hit Julius II. He refrained. The Pope represented Christ on earth and he would not commit the sacrilege.

"Finish it," the Pope ordered. "I am tired of artists. They are an unruly bunch." With that he turned his back on the artist and climbed down the series of ladders.

Michelangelo felt the pain of the stroke on his back. He had been humiliated by the Pope. He lay down his brush and sat on a stool.

Julius did not appreciate the work he had done, the difficulties he had surmounted, the pain he had endured on the platform. That evening Michelangelo walked home slowly. He felt broken. He had no interest in the ceiling. He would leave Rome. The Pope had humiliated him.

He told Andrea and Maria the story. Then he began to weep. "Pack my things. I will return to Florence," he said.

"You are correct," Maria told him. "You have taken too much abuse. The Sultan of Turkey would appreciate your gifts."

"I will not spend another hour in this blighted city."

"I will go with you," Andrea said. "Leave the ceiling unfinished. It will mock the meanness and the arrogance of the Pope."

The three of them had never been more certain of a decision in their lives.

There was a knock on the door. Maria went and opened it. A papal messenger stood at the entrance.

"Who are you and what do you want?" she asked angrily.

"I come from the Pope."

"Then you are not welcome."

"I must see Michelangelo."

"Very well. I let you in with reluctance."

The messenger stood before Michelangelo.

"Well what do you want?" Michelangelo asked.

"The Pope asks you to forgive him. He behaved like a boor," he said simply.

"He has my forgiveness," Michelangelo said.

"He wishes to remove the scaffolding so that people can admire your work. It will be assembled again. He also sends you a gift of five hundred ducats."

"Very well. It will give me time to think. I need fresh ideas."

Now Michelangelo remained at home and began to prepare the final frescoes. One night as he was working at the great table, there was a knock on the door. Maria opened it and Raphael entered.

"Well?" said Michelangelo, looking at him fiercely.

"I have seen your work. It is magnificent beyond words. There is no greater artist in the world. I was bad-mannered towards you, and come to ask your pardon."

"Thank you. I am familiar with your work. You will be long remembered and long honoured."

"You will be remembered as the greatest of all, even greater than da Vinci."

No further words passed between them. They grasped each other by the hands and looked into each others' eyes. Then Raphael turned and left the room.

Michelangelo looked at Andrea and Maria. Tears of joy ran down his cheeks.

CHAPTER 9

War broke out. Michelangelo was in the workshop working on a cartoon when Andrea rushed in.

"I saw the army moving out of the city. The Pope is leading them," he told his master.

"What nobles were with him?

"The Duke of Urbino and others I did not recognise."

"And where are they bound?"

"Ferrara."

Michelangelo went to the window and looked out.

"What shall we do now?" Andrea asked.

"I do not know. I have no directives from the Pope," he told him.

"There is a block of marble in the garden. You have an outline drawn on it. You should begin work on it."

"And what of the ceiling? That must be finished.

Trust a war to intervene. Will my troubles ever be at an end! Have you been to the Chapel?"

"Yes. The scaffolding has never be rebuilt. It lies by the wall of the Sistine chapel."

"And above it stands an unfinished ceiling. The Pope should have left me some directives."

Andrea knew that frustration was eating the mind of Michelangelo, so he decided that he would work on the marble. Like Michelangelo, it was his calling and the fresco work had interrupted his vocation.

He brought his bag of tools from the house and set them out in a row. It was a ritual with him before he began his work. They had not been used for two years. He tested their balance. Then, taking the heaviest chisel and a wooden mallet, he began to work.

Michelangelo entered the yard and sat on a bench. He studied his young apprentice at work. The boy was happy. He liked the medium of marble. He began working on the block. White chips began to fall to the ground.

"You are too eager, take it easy. Get the feel of the stone. Work with it and not against it," Michelangelo advised.

Soon Andrea fell into the rhythm of the work. At midday he took a rest. The sun was beating down on Rome. The walls were absorbing the heat. Later he went indoors and had a siesta.

In the evening Andrea began his work again. He did not feel the time passing. The sun moved across the sky and the shadows lengthened. Then it was night. The lanterns were lit. They gave out a muted light. Maria served the night meal. Then she came and sat with them. They spoke of many things and wondered what the outcome of the new war would be and how it would affect their work. Maria's older brother had joined the army and she was worried about his safety.

"He is a foolish young man," she told them. "He should have stayed in the masons' square with the others. But he wishes to win glory. Instead he may be killed."

"He will return," Michelangelo assured her. "He will grow tired of war. I have been to the battlefields and I have studied the slain. There is nothing sadder than the useless death of young men."

It was late when they retired.

The next day they fell into the rhythm of work again, Michelangelo on the cartoons for the central panel of the chapel, Andrea on the block of white marble. Michelangelo read the majestic line from the Bible again and again: *Let us make man to our own image and likeness*.

The words haunted him. Out of these words he created his cartoon. Neither Maria nor Andrea had ever seen such a noble composition. Adam was young, beautiful and without blemish. He lay in repose, with arching back, on the side of a hill and stretched his hand towards God. God, in turn, stretched his hand towards him. They resembled each other but God was older, wiser and carried a grey beard. About him billowed a red cloak and in his arm lay Eve, timid and shy.

"That is the noblest cartoon that you ever created," Maria commented. "Both God and Adam are perfect in every way."

"It is a pity that the scaffolding is not in place," Michelangelo told her. "I must do something about it."

"What can you do?"

"I will visit the Pope."

"That is dangerous; there is a war on."

"I understand but I must take the chance. Andrea can continue with his statue. Every day he improves. Prepare my travelling bag. I will leave tomorrow."

He set out alone for Bologna, but could not meet the Pope, who was surrounded by enemies and in great danger. On the edge of the battlefield lay a military camp to which the wounded were carried. The sun beat down upon them and they called for water. There was little the doctors could do for them. As he moved through the rows of wounded figures, he heard a weak voice calling to him.

"Michelangelo! It is I, Riccardo, the son of Giovanni the mason."

He stood beside the wounded figure of Riccardo. He had been wounded in the chest and the wound was suppurating. He had seen such injuries before. If they remained neglected, the poison would enter the body.

Michelangelo knew something of medicine. He examined the wound. Then he took brandy and washed it out.

"I must burn to cure," he told Riccardo.

He reddened a dagger in the fire until it glowed. Then he cauterised the raw wound. Riccardo cried out in pain and fainted. When he awoke he was on a bed of hay in a cart which Michelangelo was pushing. Above him he could see the beautiful arc of sky. Only the sound of bird song filled the air.

"You have saved me, Michelangelo. How can I thank you?"

"Return to your chisel and mallet. You are a mason. Stick to your trade."

After a slow journey of many days they arrived at Rome. By now Riccardo was in a fever.

Maria looked at his pale face. "Will he die?" she asked.

"Had he remained on the battlefield he would certainly have died. But there is some hope for him. He must be placed in a bed and covered with heavy blankets, despite the hot weather. He will sweat out the fever which is raging within him."

Riccardo lay between life and death for a week. Maria sat beside him and gave him pure water to drink.

Then one day the fever broke. He awoke and looked about him. He was still very weak but he had begun to take the first steps towards recovery.

Giovanni the stone mason wept when his son began to walk about the room. "How can I thank you, Michelangelo?" he asked.

"You have already thanked me. You have put up with me in my vile humours. You have befriended me in Rome."

Life returned to normal. Michelangelo supervised Andrea's work. Each evening he gave the boy advice and discussed the best manner of approaching the figure which was emerging from the marble. "You have the gift. Others possess the craft but you have the gift. Soon you will have to polish your statue with pumice. It will give it a patina and seal it forever. That is the best time of all. The task is finished and you caress it with pumice."

Each day news of the war was carried to the workshop. Fortune had not favoured the Pope. His enemies were gathering about him. One day a messenger arrived from the battlefield with a purse of money for Michelangelo. He was ordered to put up the scaffolding and continue with the ceiling. There was great jubilation in the workshop when the news was received.

The carpenters assembled the scaffolding,

Michelangelo supervising its erection in the Sistine Chapel beneath the barrel-shaped ceiling. Then it was time to begin his work again. His mind was fresh and rested, his imagination fired with new ideas.

They worked long hours on the new fresco. It possessed a magnificence and confidence which the other panels lacked. Time passed quickly for them on the platform. They worked in close rhythm. This rhythm had been built up over the months and years they had worked on the ceiling.

"Man was never more noble, truly a work of God. And God has never been more compassionate. He stretches a kindly hand towards His greatest creation," Andrea commented.

"That is what I had in mind from the beginning. I am pleased with the result. It binds all the other panels together," Michelangelo told him.

Meanwhile, on the battle front the fortunes of the Pope seemed to be at their lowest. Every prince and king stood against him. He was aging rapidly. He was in bad health and he had to be transported from place to place in an ox cart. He lost everything during the campaign: his army, his baggage train, his power to command men. The inhabitants of Bologna destroyed the bronze statue of Julius which Michelangelo had cast with so much difficulty.

The Pope made his way to Rome with the remnants of his army. Even the Roman nobles had turned against him. They planned and plotted behind his back.

"It is time for him to step down," they said. "We need a Pope who is pious and who prefers the church to the field of battle. He should spend more time on his knees than in the saddle of a war horse."

Michelangelo listened to all the rumours and

gossip. He gave no opinion on political matters. He had become obsessed by the ceiling and he felt that it would soon be finished. He had almost achieved the impossible.

One day, as they sat on the platform eating a simple meal, they began talking about the politics of the city.

"You should visit Julius," Maria suggested. "He is alone now and needs friends."

"Why should I? I have been alone on this platform for three years. When he did visit me it was to abuse and beat me," he retorted.

"He has been the patron of artists. He has brought them to the city, he has kept them employed. It is your Christian duty to visit him," Andrea said.

"You are both against me," Michelangelo laughed. "Very well, I will visit him. The charity of God demands that I should."

That evening he made his way along the corridors of the Vatican Palace to visit the Pope. He noticed how strangely empty the place was. Even the cardinals and the bishops were avoiding Julius. He knocked at the door of the Papal apartments and was allowed immediate entry.

The Pope was sitting on an armchair, cushioned with soft sheepskins. He looked old and worn. His eyes lacked lustre and his cheeks were netted with purple veins.

Julius looked up and gazed at Michelangelo. The artist bowed before him and he gave him his blessing.

"How is your work proceeding?" he asked.

"Very well."

"Will I be pleased with it?"

"I believe you will."

"Then I shall go and inspect it."

"Perhaps you are too weak."

"Never underestimate me. That is what my friends and enemies have done. Give me a hand."

Michelangelo took the Pope's elbow and eased him out of the armchair. Julius took his stick and shuffled slowly out of his apartments.

"I shall not strike you with it. I am too old and too feeble," he smiled.

Both men began to laugh.

They made their way slowly along the corridors.

"This place is as empty as the grave," the Pope told him. "Even my palace staff have left me. They expect me to surrender to my enemies and to call a conclave which will elect a new Pope. But they do not know the hard material out of which I am made. I am like one of your marble statues."

Eventually they reached the chapel. Andrea was cleaning up after the day's work. Michelangelo directed him to light several lanterns to show the Pope the way to the platform. Slowly and with heavy breath he drew himself painfully ceilingwards. He had to stop after every third step and take a rest. His breathing was charged with phlegm. He coughed it up from his chest and spat it onto the floor.

Finally he reached the platform. He sat down on a stool. He studied the panels with a critical eye. For a long time he remained silent. Then he looked at Michelangelo. "Do you believe that God is this kind and this compassionate?" he asked, pointing at the Creation of Adam.

"I believe he is."

"Then I can rely on his mercy."

Julius studied the ceiling once more. "You have achieved the impossible," he said. "Nobody has ever created anything more noble. The work of Raphael is beautiful. But your frescoes are sublime."

"You flatter me, your Holiness."

"I speak the truth. You merit such praise." He got up from the chair and made his way slowly down the ladders. Michelangelo helped him. When he returned to the platform, Andrea said to him, "The mark of death is upon him. He may not live to see the completion of the chapel."

"Then we must continue to work quickly."

The Pope recovered slightly. Then, while hunting outside Rome he contracted malaria. Soon he would die. He was abandoned by those close to him. The great power which he once wielded was passing from his hands. He lay on his bed like a corpse. As he lay dying, the members of his household and many others stole the furniture and valuables from his apartments. The rooms stood empty and bleak.

Andrea watched in disbelief as servants and priests entered the Pope's apartments and stole his possessions before his very eyes. The old man was too weak to move. Andrea told Michelangelo what he had seen.

"They have sacked the Papal apartments, even the curtains have been stolen."

"If he dies, the ceiling will never be finished. We must hurry," his master said.

When Maria heard what had happened, she hastened to the Vatican. She made her way to the Pope's apartments. The old man lay alone in his great bed barely breathing. She took a warm towel and bathed his face. Then she gave him thin soup.

"It is terrible what they have done," she said angrily. "I will take care of your health. I will lock the apartments and permit no one to enter."

She found two soldiers still faithful to the Pope. She

set them on guard in front of the great doors. She thought it possible that the Pope would die, but she would make his final days comfortable. She changed his sheets and freshened the room with flowers. She threw the windows open and let fresh air in. She wiped malarial sweat from his brow.

Then, slowly, the Pope began to inch back from death. His strength began to return. Each day Maria fed him with simple food.

"Do not tell them that I improve," the Pope warned her. "We must keep it a secret for the moment. I have a surprise in store for those who abandoned me. They will regret the day they plundered my apartments. You are a true Christian. I have learned much during my illness."

Only Michelangelo and Andrea knew that the Pope had recovered. They listened to the rumours circulating about Rome. The nobles boasted that they would throw the Pope's body into the Tiber. He would never rest in Saint Peter's basilica.

Then one day the Pope appeared in his papal robes in the new Saint Peter's. There was consternation in Rome. The nobles fled and cardinals and bishops sheepishly returned to the corridors outside the Papal apartments. They were received coldly by the Pope.

Thereafter, Michelangelo never had to worry about money for the commission. The Pope was most generous to him, and Maria was invited to prepare the Papal meals.

The months passed. Day by day Michelangelo worked on the ceiling. The Separation of Land from Water was complete and they commenced with the Creation of Sun, Moon and Planets.

One day, at long last, they had an end in sight. It only remained to paint the Separation of Light from Darkness. Michelangelo turned to Andrea and said, "We have been four years in this confined place. You are no longer a boy but a young man. You have mastered the technique of fresco painting and you have become a sculptor. In years to come you will bring your children to this place and you will show them the ceiling and you will say 'I learned my craft working between heaven and earth with that cantankerous man Michelangelo.' They will laugh and they won't believe you for we have done an incredible thing!"

There was a new eagerness to finish the chapel. Despite his enthusiasm, Michelangelo's strength seemed to fail him.

"He seems to lack energy. Should you not take over for him or perhaps invite Raphael or someone else to help him?" Maria asked.

"No. He is a proud man. He must finish it alone. He must draw the last line and apply the final colours."

Even the Pope was getting impatient. "Will you ever be finished, my friend? It is time to take down the scaffolding."

"Another month and it will be completed," Michelangelo replied.

But the month passed by and it was not completed. Then one day when Maria mounted the platform she discovered Michelangelo lying on the platform.

"Has he had a turn?" she asked Andrea.

"No. He studies his work. He has completed the Sistine Chapel."

"I do not believe it!" she said in awe. "You mean to say that the great work has ended?"

"Yes. He has finished. Soon the world will gaze upon our work in awe. They will ask if he had been helped by angels."

Maria felt that this was a sacred moment. She stood silently on the platform and looked at the most magnificent thing ever painted by man. She had been part of the great endeavour.

They sat and talked beneath the vast spread of the ceiling until midnight. They spoke of the time when Bramante had constructed the platform and almost destroyed their endeavour and of the first effort which had failed. They recalled the long days of summer when the chapel became a furnace and the hard days of winter when their fingers froze and became chapped.

Then it was time to leave. They took one final look at the ceiling before descending the scaffolding to the floor. Michelangelo was the last to leave the scaffold. They locked the door and walked home. It was late and Rome was almost deserted. They met some drunks who were singing of lost love and the passing of time.

The next day Andrea returned to the scaffolding and collected the materials and instruments of their trade. He took some of the cartoons and burned them. But he kept the cartoon of the Creation of Man for himself. It was something he had helped assemble piece by piece. It was too beautiful to consign to the fire.

He descended the ladders for the last time. They were stained with years of paint and carried the multicolored footprints of boots.

It took them a week to remove the scaffolding. Already there was a rumour about Rome that Michelangelo had been helped by angels in his task, that they had visited him at night and held his arms when they were tired. Some artists who visited the chapel noted what had been created and stated that they had looked upon a new wonder of the world.

When the scaffolding had been finally removed, Andrea visited the chapel with Michelangelo. They brought with them the old man. He had never been to the Vatican before and feared that he might meet the Pope.

"It would be too much for my heart to bear," he told them as he was brought in a cart to the chapel.

He stood in the middle of the chapel supported by Maria and his daughter, and looked at the ceiling. "It is a very great thing you have done. And the flood is perfect. I've been at sea and I know. I can feel the wind blow."

Andrea looked up at the magnificent achievement. He had been there on the first day when the ceiling was as empty as a desert. Now it teemed with divine and human life. He lay on the floor and looked at the miracle he had helped create. Everything was in proportion and perfectly balanced. It could not be surpassed. "God is no insignificant thing and neither is man," he remarked.

"You are correct," a voice said. It was that of Julius who now stood beside Michelangelo. He looked at the ceiling he had commissioned. "So the work has finally come to an end," he said.

"You mean the slavery has come to an end," Michelangelo replied. "I am free from this work."

"And are you free from Julius?" the Pope asked.

"I am never free from Julius," Michelangelo replied.

"Will you be present when I formally bless your work?"

"No. I have done what was expected of me."

"And where shall you go?"

"I do not know. But I will certainly leave Rome. I am tired of the city."

"And who have you brought with you?" he asked when he saw the old man.

"A friend who has stood by me during the turbulent years."

The old man's mouth was open in amazement.

"Then shall I give you all my blessing?"

They knelt down and the Pope, who had been both tormentor and friend, blessed them. Before they left the chapel, they looked at their work once more.

When they reached home they sat in the walled garden and had a small feast. Michelangelo invited many of those from the quarter who had often called to see him during the long and tedious years. They reminisced about all that had happened during that time.

The old man could not be contained. He spoke of his meeting with the Pope. It had been the highlight of his life.

"And what will you do now that the great work is finished?" Giovanni asked.

"Leave this city and wipe its dust off my feet. Perhaps I will return to Florence or move on to Carrara. I need open air and wide spaces."

"And what of Andrea?" Maria asked.

"There is no more I can teach him. He should remain in Rome. He is now a friend of the Pope's. He has already granted him a small commission."

There was a gasp of admiration from the crowd. "So you are a friend of the Pope's," they said.

"And what of Maria?" they asked.

"She has been offered work in the papal household. She remained with the Pope when others had fled. She nursed him back to health," Michelangelo explained.

"You know the high and the mighty, Michelangelo," the old man said.

"I prefer to be with my friends," Michelangelo replied, raising his wine glass and toasting their health.

At the end of the week they closed the house. Andrea had rented rooms in the masons' square and Maria had an apartment at the Vatican. They stood at the gate of the house as Michelangelo mounted an old black horse he had purchased. He carried with him his battered travelling bags. He waved to them, passed around a corner, and was gone. His work in Rome had come to an end.

CHAPTER 10

Time, like the fine wheels of God, had turned. Now Michelangelo was a very old man. Despite hardship, hard work, and the lack of sleep and food, he had reached the ripe age of eighty-nine. He was now the most famous artist in Italy. He had returned to Rome and had continued his work in the city. He had been called to improve on Bramante's design for Saint Peter's. He had carved great statues and he had designed magnificent buildings. Even in old age he continued to work.

Julius II was long since dead. Bramante had never finished his task and Raphael had died in his prime. Michelangelo never finished the famous tomb. The great white blocks which he had hewn from the cliffs of Carrara had long since been sold. All his friends were dead. Those whom he had known during the heady days in Florence were now just names on tombstones. He could look back upon a life which straddled two centuries. His art had changed the known world.

Yet even at eighty-nine there were continued demands on his time.

The vaulting of Saint Peter's was causing trouble and he had to deal with the problem. He possessed all the ills that the old usually have. He urinated with difficulty. His body was wracked with pain. He moved stiffly.

"My mind is as sharp as a razor, sharper than the minds of the young men about me, but my body fails and that is a terrible thing."

Despite his age, he kept up a lively correspondence with people. He kept in constant contact with Andrea. They wrote frequently to each other during the years. Maria sent him his favourite wine and marzolini cheese which he relished. His letters were filled with praise for her choice of wines and cheese.

Andrea was now middle-aged and possessed his own workshop in Florence. He had travelled to France and had crossed the Channel to England. He married Maria.

One day she brought him a letter from Michelangelo. "I note that his hand-writing grows weaker," she observed. "The messenger told me that his health fails. We should go and visit him."

"Yes, I think we should visit him. We have not been in Rome for a long time and a cardinal there has offered me a commission."

Maria called her servants and told them to prepare for the journey. They set off for the city on two magnificent horses. Along the road they stayed at the best inns and during the journey they reminisced on a past which had been worthy and full of excitement.

When they arrived in Rome they heard that Michelangelo was dying. A week before he had been hacking away at a piece of sculpture, determined to finish it. They rushed to his apartments. His eyes lit up when he saw them enter.

"Ah, my oldest friends have come to visit. You come in time. Life slips from me. One cannot live forever and I am prepared to depart. Yet there is much which remains to be done."

"I brought you your favourite wine and cheese," Maria told him.

It cheered him a little. She poured him some wine and held it to his lips. Then he turned to Andrea. "I have a commission to complete. I do not think I shall be able to finish it."

"Fear not – I will attend to it," Andrea assured him.

Maria sat by his simple bed. She spoke of her family. They too were artists. One had already finished his first commission and her daughter had married into the nobility. Later she went into the kitchen and prepared a light soup. She carried it to him and urged him to eat it.

"You fed me when I worked on the Sistine Chapel and now you feed me on my death bed."

"Do not talk. You will eat and then you will sleep," she urged.

"I will soon have all eternity in which to sleep. I wish Andrea to carve my tomb and I wish you to testify to my will," he told her.

"I will do all these things after you have slept," she told him.

When he awoke he dictated his will. It was short and simple: "I commend my soul to God. I commend my body to the earth. Anything of value I possess I leave to my relations. That is all."

It was cold in Rome and they kept the large fires burning. But, despite the heat, Michelangelo's body grew cold. Maria and Andrea were beside him when he died on the seventeenth of February 1564 after a long and fruitful life.

All Rome mourned his departure. He was buried in the Chapel of Santi Apostoli. The cardinals, bishops and artists of Rome came to pay their last respects. They realised what an important man they laid to rest in the sacred city. But the Florentines in the company were not pleased with the idea that the remains of Michelangelo should remain in Rome. Neither was Duke Cosimo of Florence.

"He will not rest easy in a city he never loved. He was abused here during his middle years," they said to each other.

"He must return to Florence," Andrea said.

"Do you expect us to steal his body?" one of his friends asked.

"That is what Duke Cosimo wants. That is what I want. That is what everybody in Florence expects from us."

They laid their plans. That night Andrea and many friends from Florence made their way to the Church of Santi Apostoli and removed the body from the grave. They wrapped it in a bale of cloth and, under cover of darkness, slipped out of Rome. A few days later they reached the city that Michelangelo had loved above every other city in Italy, Florence. All the artists and artisans of the city were there to greet his remains. A hero had returned to his own place. Here he was buried in the church of Santa Croce.

As they left the chapel, Andrea turn to Maria and said, "He rests well here. Rome did not deserve him. He was the greatest of all artists and we shall not look upon his like again." They passed down the steps and across the square.

Also by Poolbeg

Shiver!

Discover the identity of the disembodied voice singing haunting tunes in the attic of a long abandoned house . . .

Read about Lady Margaret de Deauville who was murdered in 1814 and discover the curse of her magic ring . . .

Who is the ghoulish knight who clambers out of his tomb unleashing disease and darkness upon the world?

Witness a family driven quietly insane by an evil presence in their new house . . .

What became of the hideous voodoo doll which disappeared after Niamh flung it from her bedroom window?

An atmospheric and suspense-filled collection of ghostly tales by fifteen of Ireland's most popular writers: Rose Doyle, Michael Scott, Jane Mitchell, Michael Mullen, Morgan Llywelyn, Gretta Mulrooney, Michael Carroll, Carolyn Swift, Mary Regan, Gordon Snell, Mary Beckett, Eileen Dunlop, Maeve Friel, Gaby Ross and Cormac MacRaois.

Each tale draws you into a web at times menacing, at times refreshingly funny.

Also by Poolbeg

To Hell or Connaught

by

Michael Mullen

Don't be afeard, brother! These Irish traitors will be all driven beyond the Shannon. So the masters say. There they will rot in a great prison. Sea on one side and river on the other. It is a clever scheme.

So begins *To Hell or Connaught*, a story from one of the most poignant periods in Irish history, told by Michael Mullen as only he can.

Together with thirteen-year-old Bryan O'Dwyer and his courageous mother we travel through a barren landscape of untilled fields and rotting crops, hoping to avoid the English soldiery as fever sweeps through the villages and countryside. This account of the final extinction of the Irish aristocracy, the few who stayed to defy the Parliamentary army, is told with devastating simplicity. Slavery or serfdom – a stark choice!

Yet the book is full of courage, humour and hope, and with the Black Dwarf, Captain Kavanagh and his resourceful wife, Lady Margaret, and our boy hero, Michael Mullen has peopled a thrilling tale with unforgettable characters.

Also by Poolbeg

The First Christmas

by

Michael Mullen

Daniel is ten and loves Christmas. He is a great friend of John Duffy, the local carpenter who carves the figures for the village crib.

One night before Christmas Daniel steps inside the crib and finds himself in Bethlehem just before the birth of the Christ child. He meets the shepherds and the Magi and is placed in mortal danger by Herod's murdering soldiers . . .

Michael Mullen has retold the world's best-known story with humour, freshness and excitement.